"Stories that delightfully reel you in"

CURIOUSLY,

@Cafe, Ne PHEW!, (HUGS), Hoodie$,
Trail..., Vanity, and other stories"

VINAY KOTHARI

BLUEROSE PUBLISHERS
India | U.K.

Copyright © Vinay Kothari 2023

All rights reserved by author. No part of this publication may be reproduced, stored in a retrieval system or transmitted in any form or by any means, electronic, mechanical, photocopying, recording or otherwise, without the prior permission of the author. Although every precaution has been taken to verify the accuracy of the information contained herein, the publisher assumes no responsibility for any errors or omissions. No liability is assumed for damages that may result from the use of information contained within.

BlueRose Publishers takes no responsibility for any damages, losses, or liabilities that may arise from the use or misuse of the information, products, or services provided in this publication.

For permissions requests or inquiries regarding this publication, please contact:

BLUEROSE PUBLISHERS
www.BlueRoseONE.com
info@bluerosepublishers.com
+91 8882 898 898
+4407342408967

ISBN: 978-93-6261-114-7

Cover design: Muskan Sachdeva
Typesetting: Rohit

First Edition: October 2023

Dedication

To people real and imaginary
To places near and far
To all that, that stays within us

Acknowledgments

Ken Goinn - CopyEditor

Ken your innate ability to make things better and immense generosity for the CopyEdit help me shape the final manuscript. You make me proud of what I have written.

Preface

I have often wondered if you pay a price for being curious or are rewarded for it.

Stories in this collection have been an outcome of witnessing God intended events that shape our lives. Encounters that refuse to be forgotten and need to be reflected upon, careful immersion into the experiences of others, and then amplifying them to capture the beauty and complexity that surrounds us.

When I hear an exchange between two people, physical or verbal in a cafe or at the airport - when it happens I don't know if I would write about it. At that point I witness the event unfolding and sense the emotions being expressed - but only at a later point when I rethink what transpired - I begin to wonder if what could be written about that fleeting moment.

I try to travel to as many different places as possible and interact with as many diverse people from all age groups and geographies. From Park Avenue to the cotton farming town of Tibby in northern Rajasthan - there is always a treasure hidden in the realm of others' experiences, offering glimpses into their joys and struggles. The stories serve as windows into their worlds, an intimate lens into their lives, that explore the universal threads that bind us all.

Observing others how they interact with each other - whether it is an uncle and a nephew within the confines of a car on a long road trip or a middle-aged woman getting trapped in the delusional fantasies of a young girl at a cafe or how a man connects with a beautiful young stranger sitting next to him on an airplane. Each incident unfurls a miniature universe, the central character in each of these narratives draws me closer, and with whom I begin to build an intimate relationship, and then the words begin to flow.

Deciding what to write about in particular is often unclear to me. At times as I begin to write, I know the beginning of the story with no clue as to how it will end. But gradually it all starts to come together. I try my best to do it justice if I decide to write about it.

In my teen years, I wrote a short story that received favorable responses from my English composition teacher and a local newspaper editor. The teacher had found my writerly style curious. The editor had found the pieces generally pleasing and had advised me if I had something to say - I should continue to write.

That was the first cut I had made as a writer, and it filled with me a belief that at some point in my life, I would develop this skill.

This encouragement to continue to write, back then, had sowed the seed. I began looking for clues, uncovering stories beneath stones, what truly lay behind when people conversed with one another, and how they chose to live their lives.

I began by writing in tidbits, personal short stories, one-sided fantasies, and confessional responses to the world around me. I dealt with what I saw and felt — my lens was tainted with bias and preference. I was partial to human emotion, how humans connected, and the small stuff that they were driven by. But I made every attempt to keep my ethos simple and atmosphere honest.

There is a great flip side to this too. As a writer, it has always been difficult, to be honest and do justice to narratives about family or friends, people who are close to you, who have the biggest impact on you, as several biases tend to creep into the writing.

I had spent a month in the summer of 2023, with a dear friend in Florida and when I decided to write about my time with him - my observations of a single aging man facing the last quarter of his life having only his fourteen-year-old dog as his companion. The outcome did not fare well. I had always known him to be objective and trusted his maturity to be open to looking at his own life critically through the eyes of another. I excitedly presented the piece for his review. But to my horror, he was deeply offended by my characterization of his life and his situation and how I had written about it. He sent me a brief message thanking me for being my inspiration following which he cut all ties and refused to respond to any of my messages thereafter. I tried to convince him over several exchanges not to lose objectivity and I saw my will end. But gradually it all starts to come together. I try my best to do it justice if I decide to write about it.

In my teen years, I wrote a short story that received favorable responses from my English composition teacher and a local newspaper editor. The teacher had found my writerly style curious. The editor had found the pieces generally pleasing and had advised me if I had something to say - I should continue to write.

That was the first cut I had made as a writer, and it filled with me a belief that at some point in my life, I would develop this skill.

This encouragement to continue to write, back then, had sowed the seed. I began looking for clues, uncovering stories beneath stones, what truly lay behind when people conversed with one another, and how they chose to live their lives.

I began by writing in tidbits, personal short stories, one-sided fantasies, and confessional responses to the world around me. I dealt with what I saw and felt — my lens was tainted with bias and preference. I was partial to human emotion, how humans connected, and the small stuff that they were driven by. But I made every attempt to keep my ethos simple and atmosphere honest.

There is a great flip side to this too. As a writer, it has always been difficult, to be honest and do justice to narratives about family or friends, people who are close to you, who have the biggest impact on you, as several biases tend to creep into the writing.

I had spent a month in the summer of 2023, with a dear friend in Florida and when I decided to write about my time with him - my observations of a single aging man facing the last quarter of his life having only his fourteen-year-old dog as his companion. The outcome did not fare well. I had always known him to be objective and trusted his maturity to be open to looking at his own life critically through the eyes of another. I excitedly presented the piece for his review. But to my horror, he was deeply offended by my characterization of his life and his situation and how I had written about it. He sent me a brief message thanking me for being my inspiration following which he cut all ties and refused to respond to any of my messages thereafter. I tried to convince him over several exchanges not to lose objectivity and I saw my own life headed towards how his life is, but with little success. I wonder if I would react similarly to someone if they had written about me - it is hard to remain neutral when faced with certain truths about others and what we see of ourselves in others. However, I will never apologize for I had no ill intention behind what I had written. I had written the story with empathy as my guide and if it comes at a cost so be it.

Writing provides a certain legitimacy to my thoughts, I have discovered a certain strength through writing which I cannot find in the volubility of speech. It lets me take on more risks. Writing makes me more courageous. Every time I write, I reveal a little more about myself, revealing age-old secrets and coming face to face with certain truths about myself.

My goal as a writer is to be able to make language do what I wish to. Enchanted by linguistic eloquence and the symphony of words to paint scenes, evoke emotions, and the ability of well-crafted sentences to transport readers to different worlds with precision and passion, I strive to achieve flawless poised prose that the reader savors. To be able to raise a reader's eyebrow with a quick turn of phrase!

The current repertoire of tales I have crafted will take your imagination to places you may have been or may not have been to, and as you read I hope the essence of the stories will linger long after you have read the final sentence.

Contents

Ne Phew!	1
(HUGS)	15
"Liv" orno	29
Touch*	39
^Vanity	55
"Mubarak"	77
?Answer	97
@Cafe	115
Hoodie$	139
___TrAIL	153
About The Author	*169*

Ne Phew!

A wedding in the family brings the unlikeliest of travel companions together.

A fifty-year-old Uncle and a seven-year-old Nephew embark upon a journey of four hundred kilometers together.

The journey begins with delays, excess baggage, extended goodbyes, last-minute frantic food preparations, and a few emergency purchases. Four adults, a child, and a driver are to travel in a spacious GLE 350. The part-minivan, part-truck-like vehicle can accommodate five passengers comfortably, with the possibility of cramming two additional passengers in the cargo seat.

The Uncle surveys the spacious car and its passengers and is delighted. Besides the front-row driver seats, there is a second row of passenger seating and an additional seating in the cargo area in the trunk.

In all likelihood, the Uncle hopes he will get to sit in the comfort of the empty passenger seat next to the driver — the three adults in the second row and the Nephew in the trunk. The young Nephew could occupy one of the two cargo seats, giving him ample space to spread his toys and spill his meals on the second seat, if he so wishes to.

Kids love the rear seats in the trunk, but an adult who has to sit on those cargo seats has to pack it in tightly. With little room to spread one's legs and little headroom, inadequate cooling on a hot summer day can make a six-hour journey hard to endure.

As the Uncle is about to board, the Nephew proposes that he wants the Uncle to sit with him in the rear seat. The Nephew is traveling for the first time without being accompanied by his mother, who is pregnant and cannot endure the length of the road trip. Bearing this fact in mind, the Uncle must oblige, as he is aware of the fact that he has to do his best to keep the young Nephew in good spirits for the entire course of the trip.

According to the Nephew, the ride is going to be carloads of fun. He suddenly displays a newly acquired fondness for the Uncle.

At the insistence of the Nephew, the Uncle much against his will complies. He even feigns a willingness and exhibits affection and happiness at the seven-year-old's proposition. It is a *family* vacation of sorts, so why not? The Uncle decides to go along with it and crawls into the rear seat.

The journey begins with a whirlwind of questions from the Nephew. The Nephew bombards the Uncle with a series of never-ending inquiries that seem to flood his curious young mind. He needs to know the why and the what, the when, the where, and the how of anything and everything he sets his eyes on.

Why are the leaves on the trees green?

Why is the sun yellow?

Is the sun much bigger than the Earth?

What is the red spot on the Uncle's finger, and will it ever go away?

How many villages will they have to pass?

And his overarching concern about how many more hours will it take to reach.

The questions are in quick succession. Before the Uncle can think of an appropriate answer, the Nephew is onto the next question. It becomes quite evident that the Nephew is only interested in asking questions and cares little about their answers. The Nephew neither acknowledges nor understands the response to anything he asks. Soon, the Nephew decides to introduce his Uncle to the various scratches, bruises, and insect bites on the different parts of his body.

Then, without waiting for consolation or empathy, the Nephew summons the Uncle to inspect the contents of the two backpacks he is carrying. The backpacks are full of toys and books, stuff to make the time on this road trip fly by. The Nephew, himself has handpicked the contents of the two bags.

Quriously

The gadgetry includes an iPad with built-in apps and games, an old non-working phone, and a fidget spinner. There are activity books, coloring books, sticker books, sketch pens, crayons, and sheaths of scribble paper. There is even greeting card stock, in the event the tiny adult might want to design and fabricate a greeting card for an unplanned occasion that he might discover along the way. A couple of card games, Spit and MonoDeal, are also stacked in the front pocket of the backpack.

The Uncle is amazed at the Nephew's ability to manoeuvre through his books, toys, and devices. Doing a little math, the Uncle concludes that it is almost mandatory to shift the Nephew's short attention span every ten minutes to a new activity. This way, the Nephew remains engaged and challenged throughout the journey - lest the unthinkable should happen: a tantrum demanding an immediate return to go home to be with his mother.

However, the Nephew turns out to be the king of inconsistency. Before the games can begin, he demands a MOSBito patch to ward off a possible sting from an errant mosquito that might by chance, enter the car. Once the protection is in place, demands to play a card game, *Spit*. The Uncle has never played the game before and is reluctant to learn the rules, so he tries to suggest reading a book. The Nephew does not want the suggestion and continues to eagerly explain the simple rules of the card game. The long stretch of the journey is an exercise in killing time, so the Uncle gives in. The moment the Uncle agrees, the Nephew changes the game to *MonoDeal*.

The Uncle tries to explain to the Nephew that he is maybe too young to truly comprehend the concepts of debt collectors, deal-breakers, and forced deals that *MonoDeal* abounds in. Besides, the game also requires the spreading of several cards on a table or an equivalent flat surface. As the Nephew starts to deal he realizes there is limited space to spread the playing cards in the trunk, so he switches back to *Spit*. They play a single round, and then the Nephew has a sudden urge to want to paint in his brand new Water Wow - a watercolor coloring book. Within minutes, after making a couple of brush strokes, he switches to a magnetic puzzle book. For the next thirty minutes, he tries several activities, but none can hold his attention for more than a few minutes.

There is a vibrant world of life outside the car window. The Uncle invents a new game that he thinks the Nephew might enjoy. He calls it "First to see New." The Uncle, while trying to explain the rules of the game to the Nephew, realizes the idea is falling on deaf ears. It is becoming apparent to the Uncle that the Nephew will not listen to any of his suggestions as to how he needs to occupy the time.

The Uncle observes the Nephew possesses a constant need to be entertained, talked to, or given attention. If it is not books, then it's gadgetry. If not gadgetry then it is a need to recite a recently learned poem. Soon the poem is forgotten for a meal request!

And with meals, his inconsistency rises to a new, higher level. Satisfying the Nephew's snacking requests is no easy task. A lot of food options have been provisioned for, by the grandmother and the mother. Sweet, salty Bombay mixes, salted cashews, pistachios, Turkish baklava, Mejdool dates, cold-pressed pomegranate juice, sliced mango in lock-tite boxes, an assortment of Belgian chocolates, candy of all sorts - all stacked in two sizeable plastic mesh picnic baskets. The Nephew immediately rejects most of the food offered, refusing to eat anything. It takes a lot of coaxing and explaining by the Uncle to convince him to feed himself.

The Nephew begins by liking fruit; the next minute, he hates fruit. He is offered a sandwich but asks for potato chips instead. With the very first bite of a chip, he complains it is not the right flavor. He likes chocolates, then he hates them. Fresh fruit juice, which has been packaged especially for him for the road trip, is turned down. He wants a soda instead. He often punctuates his food requests with an unpleasant, long, high-pitched whine. Rest assured, no matter which food item is at issue, it is always wrong. He may have liked it in the past, but not today.

Amid the shifting demands, the trunk space is soon littered with wrappers, partially melted gummy bears on the seats and the carpet below, and flakes of chips, cookies, and bread crumbs. Fruit juice has found a way onto the seat and the Nephew himself. The Nephew is now a bundle of food morsels and repulsively sticky to the touch. The Nephew smells gluey, feels gummy, and tastes syrupy. All the Uncle can think of is a pail of water, and a towel to wash the Nephew, until he is clean head to toe. The

Nephew wipes himself vigorously with wet wipes while constantly reiterating "it is good to be clean." To stay germ-free, he uses some hand sanitizer, which he always carries in the side pocket of the backpack.

A full belly after a meal of different foods might be expected to result in the Nephew taking a nap. The Uncle hopes that as the Nephew sleeps, he can use the remaining time to continue reading his unfinished book. Unfortunately, the high-calorie, high-sugar snack choices have fortified the Nephew, and his energy levels rise to new highs. There are now new demands.

Growing up in the seventies, the Uncle knew that children often had to earn the attention of elders by proper behavior or completion of prescribed chores. But the Nephew demands attention without guilt or an intention to compromise.

Three hours into the trip, with a similar amount of time still to pass, the company of the tiny adult is beginning to exceed the tolerance limit of the fifty-year-old Uncle. Also, the discomfort of the rear cargo seats is making the Uncle increasingly irritable. The

Uncle soon finds himself entering his natural state of grouchiness, typical of single men at his age. As a child-free person, the Uncle knows he has to preserve his outer calm in moments of internal turmoil and trivial annoyances by a child.

A probable solution, the Uncle reasons, is to occupy the Nephew with an activity that he can undertake by himself. The self-occupying activity will relieve the Uncle of the task of having to bestow constant attention, mandatory admiration, and display a liking for the Nephew - seemingly all requirements of the unhealthy state of modern childhood. The Uncle unzips the backpack and provides a box of crayons and a coloring book to the Nephew. He prompts the Nephew to embark on a coloring activity.

The Nephew jumps at the idea but soon suggests he has a better idea saying, "Yes! Yes!"

The Uncle wonders what now? The Nephew proclaims he wants to make a greeting card. The greeting card is to be a surprise for someone special. He demands that the Uncle keep his eyes shut, for the entire duration of the artwork's creation.

Quriously

He insists on using the card stock and the brand new 101-piece set of Mitashi Skykids Crayolas for his craftsmanship. The needed crayolas are in the trunk. This fact requires stopping the car, offloading the bags, and procuring the required materials. An attempt is made to convince the Nephew to make the card with felt pens that are in his backpack, but the Nephew will have none of it. He wants what's in the trunk, and he wants it now, he announces loudly. The Uncle can't help but conclude that the Nephew is not annoying or out of control, but he is simply a brilliant negotiator. He is a person who always gets what he wants.

The Uncle thinks "Comply with the Nephew's every wish, so that the record of no request going unfulfilled to date can be maintained."

The Uncle gestures to the driver to pull over. The driver thinks it's another needless stop, only adding to delays. But his concerns are of no consequence. The driver procures the items as commanded.

At this point, the Uncle has had enough. He expresses his desire to move to the empty seat beside the driver, which has been vacant until now. The luxury and comfort of the large bucket seat are going to waste. The seat feels like liberation, which will let the Uncle compose his mind and body and provide the necessary reboot to his attitude to make his mood pleasant.

He tries to explain to the Nephew that this will give him the required privacy that he needs for his card-making venture. However, it is not to be. The Nephew states that the Uncle shall make no such move.

The Uncle will be required to sit along with him in the rear seat with his eyes shut. No ifs, ands, or buts. It has to be his way on the highway.

The Uncle has travelled from a different city, one that is a thousand kilometers away, and is meeting the Nephew for the first time after several years. He feels it is impossible to refuse or disregard the Nephew's desires. The Uncle knows he should use his better judgment and converse calmly with the Nephew. He cannot get combative with someone less than a tenth of his age. He has to find the patience to deal with the many moods, imperious orders, self-centered behavior, and unreasonable pleadings of the child.

The Uncle is less than thrilled with the most recent directive, but caves in and bends an already aching lower back once again to occupy the back seat. The trip is quickly moving toward punishment territory for the Uncle. The Uncle is seriously wondering how he ended up here. In a situation from which there is no immediate escape.

While the Uncle sits lost in thought with his eyes shut, the Nephew asks if he can guess whom the card is for and for what occasion, if any.

The Uncle thinks that the Nephew, after a couple of hours on the road by himself, has started to miss his mother, and it is a *miss my mom card*.

Or perhaps it is a birthday card for one of his school friends.

Perhaps it is a card for the auspicious religious festival just around the corner.

Perhaps it's a get-well card for his grandfather.

The Uncle makes a few more unsuccessful guesses - all dismissed by the Nephew, with a rapid shake of his head from side to side.

Finally, the Nephew asks the Uncle to give up and unfold the palm of his hand while yelling, "Eyes shut! Eyes shut!" The Nephew places the card in the Uncle's palm and says, "It's for you."

The Uncle upon receiving the card feigns astonishment and is about to deliver thanks. But even before the Uncle can open the card, the Nephew demands another blank card paper to begin making his second greeting card.

The Nephew immediately takes on his second project. As the Uncle opens the card in his palm. The card has a big red heart on the upper fold, and it simply says, "Uncle I love you" on the bottom fold, scribbled in blue watercolor crayon. The Nephew has signed the card with a red crayon. The Nephew has paid little attention to punctuation, capitalization, or keeping the written text following an imaginary straight line.

The Uncle has just witnessed real-life magic. The discomfort of the rear seat is suddenly bearable, and the remaining three hours of the trip seem like they will pass in the blink of an eye.

A good feeling envelops the car, the road, and the miles ahead.

(HUGS)

A lex's phone buzzes and a reminder flashes — *Julio's b-day*

Alex fingers the screen to quickly type the usual happy birthday greeting and is about to press send when he pauses, will a birthday wish buzzing through a text message on Julio's phone mean much, if anything at all, to Julio. Wishes are free and overused. Julio must have received plenty of them on all his social media channels. Sometimes, but not always, wishing is a gesture of caring. But then again, wishes have little utility to the person for whom they are intended other than as a soft reminder that you exist. For Julio, a person who believes in informality, a birthday is not much of a big deal.

(HUGS)

Julio has been through the toughest year in his very young life and Alex tries to find a way to make his birthday more consequential. If Alex's life was a fairy tale and a genie had granted him three wishes, he would give one of the wishes to Julio. Now, that kind of birthday gift would carry some weight. But life is no fairy tale, Julio can attest to that!

In Julio's twenty-eighth birth year, he lost his fiancé, Janaina, to sarcoma. Julio and Janaina were both models, one fitness and the other bikini. They were a picture-perfect couple, a couple that could make you believe in happily-ever-afters. Having been together for seven Christmases, on the eighth Christmas Janaina developed a small localized lump on her left thigh, which turned out to be cancerous. Within a month, cancer seeded her lungs, metastasized to her bones, and rampaged through her liver. Once it began, Julio was by her side every minute of every day. Given Janaina's will and fortitude everyone expected Janaina to make a full recovery.

With unconditional love and undying care, Julio puts all of his hopes into prayers for Janaina. He asked, Saint Santa Muerte to shower Janaina with kindness and spare her life. But seemed like the Saint was not interested and a fatal chemo session delivered a death sentence, and Janaina succumbed to her illness. The Grim Reaper had arrived without warning and much sooner than expected. Julio's prayers had gone unanswered. Men simply lack that kind of power.

Janaina's death is agonizingly painful for Julio, so he chooses to disappear and remain quiet, still, and lost in the memory of his fiance for a while. All he wanted was to relive every memory of his time with her. He tried to fathom the reality that human life is not eternal and all the people we truly love leave us, one day. How little control, he thought we have over our lives.

But as the months went by, Julio started to pull himself together, slowly stepping out of his self-imposed exile. By the end of the first year, he had accepted that death is man's inevitable destiny and he had to learn to live with it. Having accepted his destiny, he began to adjust to the many facets of daily life, in a world without Janaina.

Two years ago, Alex and Julio had lived together for a couple of months as roommates. During that time Alex got to know Julio well. Now witnessing Julio's readiness to move on from his loss, Alex thinks that the best birthday present might be to take him on a vacation to lift his spirits.

So, Alex and Julio, bring out the adventurer in them, and set off to Quintana Roo — a Mexican state privileged by nature. It is surrounded by the beautiful Caribbean Sea. It has mangroves, jungles, cenotes, underground rivers, and lagoons. On its coast, lies the town of Tulum, southwest of the resort city of Cancún.

Hopefully, Cancún will fill the void created by Janaina's loss, and Tulum will provide the much-needed freedom from the self-repeating thoughts of Janaina that plague Julio's mind. Julio finds that both Cancún and Tulum provide a change of scene. But they also turn into fertile playgrounds, where he and Alex undertake mock combats and combative exchanges that are often required for male bonding. Spontaneity is the one quality needed for playfulness and teasing. The interactions are a blend of banter and rhetoric, physical as well as verbal. The plenty of pictures taken with their phones during the trip, become proof of the fervent camaraderie between Alex and Julio.

First, there is an episode on the hammock. Alex lies in the hammock enjoying the cool ocean breeze, swaying between the sun and the shade of the coconut trees with clear blue skies above. The hammock, handcrafted by artisans in the Yucatan, employs an ancient diamond weave with a stocky white rope. It has adjusted and molded to the weight and shape of Alex's body perfectly, creating this moment of pure bliss — a moment that does not last long.

Alex's eyes fall upon Julio walking through the gates into the resort. He is returning from the beach, after an hour-long sunbathing session lying on a chaise and braving the Mexican sun. He has the bright yellow beach towel draped on his left shoulder and is holding a bottle of Ron Con Coco in his right hand. It is a mixture of rum and coco water, repackaged in a label-less soda bottle, sold by a beach pedlar for about fifty pesos. As Julio walks towards Alex, he sips a cap full of the fermented milky liquid. He pulls back on the rope extension that ties the

(HUGS)

hammock on one end to a coconut tree and offers Alex a capful. As he hands over the cap to Alex, Julio realizes that by pulling the rope extension toward him he can increase and decrease the swing of the hammock. He begins to understand the mechanics of the hammock. Pulling the rope extension gently or firmly can alter the amplitude of the hammock swing.

Julio then begins to tug the rope extension: at first, he causes the hammock to sway gently, but soon increases the speed. Alex having lost control of the hammock, tells Julio - "Don't do that!" But Julio pays no attention to the demand and starts to swing the hammock with greater force, causing it to swing wildly back and forth between the two coconut trees from which it is suspended. Under the influence of gravity, the hammock is rotating ninety degrees in each direction from its equilibrium point. Alex does not trust the strength of the ropes that the hammock is made of. To reduce the risk of tumbling out of the hammock, he grabs the sides with both his hands and wraps the hammock around himself.

Alex is now screaming - "Stop Will you cut that out - Cut that out! - Stop! - Stop!" Julio pays no attention and seeing Alex panic, begins to laugh uncontrollably.

Julio lets the hammock oscillate at maximum amplitude and steps back to take a picture. Alex is cloaked by the hammock and wailing for Julio to stop. But for Julio, it is a PPM: picture-perfect moment.

The next PPM happens under the undeniably magical spell of the little parcel of escapist paradise called Tulum.

Alex and Julio are hundreds of miles from home. Using Google Maps, they easily find their way to the little seaside town of Tulum. Away from the beaches on a potholed side road stands a small handmade sign written in chalk that marks the entry gates for "The Cenote."

The atmosphere at the cenote is playful in spirit. Tourists swarm the place and sunbathe along with the arboreal iguanas that freely ramble on the grounds during the day. With only a few locals, the place is overrun with tourists — scantily clad French, Americans, and Caribbean Islanders. Young and old strut about wearing life jackets, snorkels, and fins. A wooden pathway twists and turns under a canopy of thick vegetation Montezuma cypresses and jacarandas line the path of the entrance to the cenote.

Alex enters the gardens at the cenote in his full-body dive skin. Julio emerges bare-chested in his board shorts, which sit far below his navel and way beyond his knees, carrying a full-face snorkel with the mouthpiece dangling from it.

Watching Alex walk towards him with his rotund belly protruding from the center of the suit, looking like a walking seal, Julio lets go of a howl of laughter.

Alex could care less. He is aware of the changes to the shape of his body that have happened with age. He defiantly struts, in a self-contained manner in the dive skin.

Alex and Julio are energized at the very first sight of the crystal-clear waters of the reservoir. Alex instantly feels that the cenote has a secret power to restore health and life. Its waters shimmer in varied shades from turquoise blue to emerald green under the spectacular beams of sunlight from the crevices in the rock overhead. It is a nice combination of open pools and caves.

The water lies beneath a gigantic limestone cave. It is cold but crisp and refreshing on a hot day.

One pool of water leads into a cove straight ahead and another to a cavern on the right. The cove houses a colony of bats while the cavern contains a turtle pool. Fish swim freely all around. A rope kept afloat with buoys leads to a cul-de-sac deeper in the cavern.

Julio and Alex stand on the edge of the platform and urge each other to take the plunge. Alex thinks it is the right moment to take pictures with the stunning backdrop. He hands his phone over to a young American, standing beside them, and asks if he will take the shot. The American takes a few steps back, flips between landscape and portrait modes on the phone several times, and tries to focus and refocus to get the perfect shot. This is taking longer than necessary for a single click.

Julio and Alex stand at the edge of a platform with fixed smiles waiting for the American to click, which is not happening soon enough. While waiting, Julio turns around and looks at Alex with a contemptuous smile. Alex responds, "Can you believe this?" Julio suddenly turns sideways, and with a swift move of his

(HUGS)

arm shoves Alex into the water. Alex falls face first, flat into the icy water, and seconds later Julio plunges and emerges right beside him.

As Julio surfaces, he holds both of Alex's shoulders with both his hands and uses his entire body weight to dunk Alex underwater. Alex resists but is no match for Julio's superior strength. Julio repeatedly dunks Alex — once, twice, three times, going at it full force to make Alex bob in and out of the water.

The commotion caused by the continuous bobbing and splashing, causes several onlookers to gather at the platform, not knowing if it is play or if someone is gasping for air while being forcibly drowned.

To the American, on the platform, all of this looks oddly familiar. He says, "Boys will be boys," and is having a gay time watching Julio roughhousing with Alex. He soon decides this is a hilarious and ideal moment for the picture he is entrusted to take. He focuses, snaps, clicks, and captures the fun, again and again.

For the rest of their time on the Yucatan, the play only gets worse. The tendency to fight in jest does not go away between the two grown men. The adrenaline rushes through them as they continue to play and tease each other all the way back to Mexico City.

As Alex later scans the pictures on his phone, he thinks, "The entire trip, Julio in the prime of his youth looked like an Aztec prince." Julio successfully combines the worst of Latin taste with the tackiness of Miami Beach. His physical frame is indescribably compelling. He sports a thick gold chain around his neck and a Yankee's baseball flipped back on his head, his dark hair peeking through the snapbacks. He carries the vacation look in every pic — always looking cool and charismatic in his way, living his life simply and not being bothered by anything. To Alex, Julio approaches life with a conquistadorian attitude.

Back in Mexico City, it is finally time to say goodbye. The two men have finished the last round of the canasta and Alex wants to thank Julio for a wonderful evening but is waiting for the right time to

(HUGS)

do so. He is not sure if Julio will come down to the lobby to see him off. So, as they stand from the card table, Alex put his sneakers on which the laces have been previously knotted, Alex merely slips his feet in. Alex thinks he will offer his thanks at the main door of Julio's apartment. Last impressions can make lasting impressions.

As Alex moves toward the door Julio says he will come down to the lobby to see him off.

As the Uber waits it is at last time to say the final goodbye. At first, Alex with both hands embraces Julio — is ever mindful, that the embrace, does not cross the decency boundary. It is a good bar embrace, not a hug.

Then it is time for Julio to say his goodbye. He gives Alex an embrace with a soft hold. The two bodies barely touch one another. The men look at each other and smile. Within seconds, Julio pulls Alex into him and holds him tight, close to him. The embrace seamlessly turns into a hug, lasting a moment longer than it should have. Julio wraps both his arms around Alex's shoulders just below the neck, too tight but with the right tenderness. Alex without hesitation, throws his arms around Julio's waist. As the two men mutter their thanks, Julio rests his head on top of Alex's shoulder. The weight of Julio's neck on his shoulder sends a wave of emotions through his body. Alex mirrors Julio's gesture by placing his head on Julio's shoulder, totally undaunted. Alex feels the skin of Julio's neck lingering so close to his lips that he cannot resist giving a quick peck. The two men maintain a prolonged embrace. They hug each other and probably share similar feelings.

This delicate dance, two bodies coalescing for a second, lingering a moment longer than necessary with arms roped around each other, leaves Alex feeling confused — What kind of a hug was this? Honest and innocent? Did it say something without actually saying it? Did he just receive the hug or did he give the hug?

The hug feels priceless like loyalty and valuable like time. He wishes he could store it and lock it up in a safe. Alex likes the fact that it happened as a simple physical gesture. Maybe it was just the Latin in Julio.

(HUGS)

It lasts only a moment, but the memory will last a lifetime. A hug after all has no material reality. It simply facilitates mutual trust between two individuals. Similar scenes happen all around the world, all the time.

"Liv" orno

Lia had longed to go to Italy for years. She had gone this summer only to return home with a greater longing to go back. For two weeks she had traveled through Lombardy, Tuscany, and Lazio and visited Milan, Rome, Florence, and Pisa. She enjoyed it all, even the intimidating entry lines at the Vatican, the melee at the Trevi fountain, and the scorching heat of the Roman sun at the Colosseum.

In the Vatican, she was in awe when she first set her eyes on Michaelangel's masterpiece, the Pieta in St Peter's Basilica. The frescos painted by Michaelangelo on the ceiling of the Sistine Chapel filled her with wonder. For her to witness human creativity at its finest was an absolute joy.

In Florence, the birthplace of Renaissance art, she felt privileged to be able to view firsthand the world-famous statue of David, the perfect man, and Botticelli's Birth of Venus. The abundance of genius squeezed into a short spell of vacation time made the experience overwhelming. It was too much too soon. An exotic, expensive fragrance had been sprayed on her soul, redolent and uplifting — but this aroma would quickly dissipate.

As the Trenitalia rolled into Florence's Santa Maria Novella train station. Lia with her bags waited to disembark by the coach door. A tall devastatingly handsome carabinieri was standing by the door and next to him, she noticed a young Italian youth leaning against the grab rail. He was the same height as she was. His wavy, disheveled blonde hair fell over his shoulders. He had a fresh, just-showered look. His skin was tan; he was in the prime of his youth. He wore knee-length khaki cargo shorts with a white popover shirt. He stood cross-legged in flat-cork summer sandals gazing out the window. Only in Italy, Lia thought, you can find beautiful men, one on every corner.

Lia was captivated by the good looks of the Italian youth, and Lia softly muttered a, "hello" - he instantly responded with a friendly "bongiorno." The innocent exchange dissolved the insurmountable distinctions between a tourist and a local. Lia sensed the spark, a spark that made her contemplate a holiday fling. Given the unlikely turn her life had suddenly taken, Lia tried to find an excuse to move the conversation forward. But then she noticed what he was wearing.

His shirt caught her eye. She started gazing at it, and he noticed.

She lied, "I like the shirt," she liked him, not the shirt.

He responded in stiff Italian, "Scuzi," taken aback by the suddenness of her compliment. Lia repeated slowly, "I like the shirt,"

The second time the English sank in and he replied, "Grazie perfetto ehh er per summer."

Lia knew he means, "Thank you, it's perfect for summer."

Lia acknowledges and adds - "Yes the shirt is beautiful."

She sized him up quickly, she was dazzled by his looks and struck by his flirtatiousness. She wondered if she should continue to play along.

But she was confused. She was smitten with him and his shirt. The shirt had had a profound impact, she continued to stare at the shirt, trying to get a better look at the fabric, the collar, and its other embellishments. The youth instead of saying thank you for her compliment offered additional information about the shirt.

"Yes - I bought it in Livorno for 4 euros"

Those simple words from the boy, regarding where and how much he bought the shirt for, fell like rose petals on Lia. She thought he was probably called Luca or Lucio, which would go so well with Lia. She continued to stare at the shirt. Feeling validated, he waited for her to say more.

Lia took a step forward to get closer to the youth and touched the fabric at the end of the sleeve and said, "It's nice."

Quriously

The train moved ever slower and finally came to a halt at the platform. Lia wanted to talk more, but to do so seemed inappropriate. She sensed his joy and serenity in wearing the shirt. As they stepped out of the train carriage, they said their "ciaos." Her eyes tried to follow him for as long as she could. The crowds of holidaymakers that seemed to abound in Italy at this time of year, swallowed him.

It had all happened too fast, and after a few minutes, she began to reexamine what had just occurred. She regretted not suggesting sipping an espresso together at a cafe but was still elated by the surprise discovery of a beautiful shirt, worn by the young boy and was proud to have recognized its beauty in an instant. All it took was a single glimpse of the shirt and she wanted it. Her desire to see centuries-old art by the masters had now been replaced by a craving to seek out a similar shirt and buy one for herself. She was confident that she could find such a shirt in the many clothing boutiques that line the cobbled streets of Florence. However, she had a problem — she could not describe it, in a meaningful way in her broken Italian, to any shirt vendor. Nonetheless, she inquired at several artisan stores and tourist trinket outlets with no success.

But she hung on to the memory of the shirt.

In a fleeting peek, the shirt had seemed to say -

"wear me for I am incredibly soft on your skin, fabricated with love and detail,

I was born in a land where turquoise waters lap gently against the sun-warmed shores, and salt-scented breezes infuse the air,

I seek much admiration,

friends will inquire,

strangers will gaze,

My simplicity will soothe,

My beauty will comfort,

I am the perfect companion for all your wanderings,

I am free-flowing, free-spirited, unfettered, uncaged."

The shirt was not an Oxford or a Polo, nor a Henley or a button-down.

It was short-sleeved, made of white cambric or probably organic cotton grown in Puglia, casual and breathable, and held in perfect shape by a web of invisible stitches.

The shirt was cut slightly loose through the body for easy "popping" on and off. It had a soft banded collar with no breast pocket or buttons, and a square hem with two side slits that made it ideal for wearing untucked.

Both sides of the plunging v-neck were hand-embroidered in intricate motifs. Birds, vines, and flowers were sowed everywhere on the white fabric around the plackets. A tasseled tie adorned the neckline.

The delicate embroidery was in muted shades of the sea, sky, and sand. The colors of the threads took you from the shimmering blues of the coastal waters to the warm yellows and fresh lavender of the Tuscan coast. The sewing was embellished with tiny blue glass crystals, seemingly more precious than sapphires.

A bestseller for a perfect day in the sun, a work of art for its immediate appeal, an appeal so understated that could be easily missed and perhaps never see its day.

Even though designed for a man, the fundamental truth of the shirt was that it had no agency with any particular gender. It was made either for a man or a woman and it was just made beautifully. Lia's phone was full of pictures of ruins of the Roman Empire and Renaissance art and architecture but held no image of the shirt. It was the simple elegance of the pristine shirt and how it was worn that drew her to it. If she did have it, not only would it be the perfect memento of her trip, but she would probably wear it more than any other piece of clothing she owned. Lia would keep it in wearable condition for as long as possible, till time would scar it with stains and tears. She could not help but fall in love with Italy - with its incredible history and unforgettable landmarks, from the perfection of the Davide in Florence to the surreal painting of the Last Supper at the Church of Santa Maria in Milan.

The desire to see the birthplace of the Renaissance and the works of Michelangelo and Leonardo had lured Lia to Italy for the first time.

The next time, Lia's singular draw to return to Italy will be to find the "Livorno Shirt" - "mia tesoro" - (her treasure), and once Lia finds it, she shall treasure it for a lifetime.

Touch*

SaiKetan is in a foul mood. It's partly because of the typical monsoon evening, with relentless showers, impossible parking, and damp clothes. But it's largely because much against his will, his girlfriend has dragged him to an adaptation of Shakespeare's *As You Like It*.

Not entirely sure what he has done to deserve this but maybe, Sai thinks, the Gods have decided to punish him tonight.

SaiKetan is a recent transplant to Mumbai from an extremely religious family in Hyderabad. Not only does he lack proficiency in English, but English theater absolutely is of no interest to him. His girlfriend reassures him that theater in Mumbai has come of age, and the plays are way more entertaining

Touch*

than what Bollywood spews out every week. She reminds him that it is a comedy, a humorous adaptation of the original, and may not be that difficult to follow. In English and a comedy? — That's two strikes against it. English comedy mixed with the rain. Sai is so flustered that he is in no mood for something light-hearted, at least not on a rainy nite.

Sai is hoping against hope that someone or something will change the course of the evening. He wonders how he can drum up the necessary enthusiasm to bear the onslaught of this two-hour-long play.

The theater smells of fresh rain. This evocative earthy smell is mixed with the odor of damp clothes and human sweat, smells that are typical on a wet rainy night. There is a large crowd, a fashionable habitué of theater-goers, a long queue at the ticket counter, and an even longer line to enter the theater. The cafe is teeming with aspiring actors, writers, and the fecund crowd of a metropolis.

The theater building houses a single auditorium painted in black. An outdoor gallery and cafe area is interspersed with cylindrical columns, and long-span steel trusses that support the roof. The walls of the gallery and cafe are not left bare — flyers written in magnificent bold fonts, advertising upcoming plays are pasted all over the walls. There is a bookstore around the corner, in a separate structure, that resembles an outhouse.

The theater has a reputation for accommodating the most exquisite collection of plays the city has to offer along with the most exceptional acting talent.

The queue to enter the theater circles twice around the gallery. SaiKetan joins the line while his girlfriend goes to collect the tickets at the counter. The people in the queue are advancing at a slow pace toward the entry door. Sai is observing, looking at, searching, even staring at the overtly cheerful crowd of twenty-somethings, all of whom are out to enjoy an evening at the theater. None of them excite him. Sai thinks he'd rather be home on a rainy Sunday evening, than at an event like this.

SaiKetan sluggishly moves in line toward the entrance. And then, *mirabile dictu*, a young boy with a baseball cap, and an older lady appear out of nowhere and pass him by. Sai catches the boy's eye; The boy piques his interest. Sai's eyes follow him as he walks down the queue.

SaiKetan begins to wonder if the boy and the lady have come to the theater tonight to watch the play or if they have just come for coffee at the cafe or to book tickets for a later show. Sai secretly hopes that they have come to watch the same play that he and his girlfriend are here to see. The boy and his lady companion go to the ticket counter first. Then the lady breaks away from the boy to visit the ladies' room and the boy is left all to himself. The boy begins to browse through all the show flyers that drape the black walls of the gallery to occupy his time.

From Sai's place in the queue, which is about thirty feet away from the boy, he notices the boy's musculature, cocksure demeanor, animated expressions, and quick reactions. The boy appears to be full of optimism and hope. The boy is comfortable in his skin and confident of the power his square, symmetrical good-looking face holds. His flawless brown skin, with its handsome and bold features, shines through his short wavy black hair.

The boy is standing just looking around and feeling a little out of his element. He does not dress like a theater aficionado — no black kurta, no shoulder bag, no beard. He is wearing a plain white v-neck t-shirt with khaki cargo shorts and brown loafers. Several beaded black bands style his left wrist. The boy's casual-chic style makes no fashion statement, but neither does it make a concession to being stylish. His attire is befitting for the season on hand.

The sudden interest in this young boy has taken hold of SaiKetan unexpectedly. He wants to deny his predilection, but it is so natural that he cannot help but indulge it. The boy has proven to be the perfect stimulant, and he takes a liking to him instantaneously.

Sai has an instant desire to get close to him, but he has to contain himself given the company he is with, lest she notice his roving eye. Sai's heart beats with lust. He no longer can suppress his desires. Things are beyond his control. The boy, however, is unaware that he has an unsuspecting admirer in near proximity or that he is currently under such detailed scrutiny.

Touch*

There is little about the boy that Sai does not like.

The boy's lady companion returns in five minutes. He greets her awkwardly and with forced politeness. His reaction leads Sai to assume that he is here to pay her back for acts of kindness that she might have bestowed upon him – an acting break, a modelling assignment, or perhaps an introduction to a high-profile director.

As they walk past, Sai catches a glimpse of him and a glimpse is enough to change his mood. As the boy and the older lady join the very end of the queue, Sai feels his evening is starting to show signs of getting better.

Unfortunately, the boy is a good forty people behind Sai. As Sai approaches the entry door he cannot help looking back a few times even while he is being ushered inside.

The theater is all black and fan-shaped. Eight rows of stadium seats with cushioned benches surround a wooden stage on three sides, amphitheater-style. The wooden floorboards creak and squeak every time someone lands a foot on them with a heavy tread. The seating is unassigned, there are no seat numbers. The number of people the theater can accommodate depends on how tightly the audience can be squeezed onto the benches. Most of the center seats on the straight benches are unavailable. Sai and his girlfriend are asked to sit in the second row from the stage, right off the entrance to the auditorium. They are seated on a curved bench that wraps around the stage. The bench can accommodate three guests maximum. Because it bends around a corner, however only the two of them are allowed to share the bench, which is meant for three. The theater is fast filling up, and very few seats remain. All the while they are being seated, Sai's eyes are fixed on the entrance in anticipation. He secretly wishes that the boy, by some freak chance, will be seated next to him. The possibility of being able to sit next to the boy for the next two hours will be the only saving grace of the evening, for he is sure the play will fail to live up to its promise.

The theater is filled to capacity in the next few minutes. Just some empty gaps remain on a few benches, speckled in undesirable locations. The theater has reached the maximum number of people it can accommodate. As the lights dim, the

Touch*

centerstage is illuminated by a single spotlight and the faces of audience members are no longer easy to make out. The darkness in the small black theater is designed to make the audience feel a part of every performance, Having audience members seated so tightly next to each other and so close to the actors adds to the intimacy of the experience. Little does Sai know that he is about to experience this intimacy first-hand.

Sai begins to wonder if the boy and his lady companion will be able to sit together. Or will they have to split up, based on available seating?

At last, Sai sees the two of them enter and walk the catwalk. Both of them look around trying to locate two adjacent seats but have no luck. They turn right and then turn into Sai's row. The usher who accompanies them asks Sai and his girlfriend to squeeze in more tightly. Sai's girlfriend complains, but Sai willingly obliges. Now there are four of them sharing a bench made for three. It is tight and close, and the boy is seated to Sai's right, right next to him.

An enormous wave of feeling wells up inside of Sai. He suddenly feels alive and terrified at the same time. He is excited, and at that very least opportune moment, his girlfriend places her hand on Sai's left hand. Sai barely even realizes the act of intimacy his girlfriend is trying to initiate. His pulse is racing with the boy seated next to him. The boy is sitting beside Sai on the curve on the bench. Given the tightness of the space, any minute now, with the slightest shift by either of them, their bodies are bound to touch one another.

They are seated unnervingly close. With the slightest shift of the boy, Sai's skin prickles at the very touch of his bare, slightly hairy knee against his. The sensation is exciting and delicious. The first touch feels like a quick kiss with pursed lips, and it turns Sai on. The boy is clueless about the emotions he is stirring up inside of Sai. Here lies the inescapable irony of open seating in an overbooked theater.

The play begins, with feisty actors whimpering lines about love and screaming their passion in frightening voices. *'Beauty provoketh thieves sooner than gold.'*

The play quickly shifts from the court of Duke Frederick to the forest of Ardenne, where the actors

Touch*

seem to escape the court corruption and deception to discover natural and free love. In Sai's distracted state, he notices how love can make some of the characters do some pretty dangerous and foolish things.

The theater is dark, and Sai is confident that his mind is transforming this Shakespearean romantic comedy into sensual erotica executed secretively and slyly. The boy has no inkling — he is focused on the play. Sai's focus has long since shifted from the play to the odd touch, which continues to happen randomly between the boy and himself.

Sai and the boy are sitting alongside each other. But a few minutes later when Sai shifts, the opposing lateral sides, Sai's right to the boy's left. From Sai's shoulder to Sai's elbow, from Sai's waist to Sai's knee touch the boy's body. Sai can ruffle the hair on the boy's thigh with the creases in his own pants. Sai is wearing a short-sleeved shirt, so the bare part of his forearm is touching the boy's bare forearm. Sai pretends to immerse himself in the play, but he is intensely engaged in the sensation of the boy's touch. The boy is unperturbed by this physicality. He does not recoil; he does not respond. He wears an expression of amazement as he continues to watch the play.

There are lines at which the boy reacts. His reaction, however, is just a nod. The boy does not clap, and seldom does he applaud.

All Sai cares about is the next brush of their skin. The touch feels fantastic. By now, Sai has completely lost track of the play.

The actor's volubility is just background noise to the imaginary fantasy that Sai has fallen prey to. Sai begins to think the boy is being receptive; that his body reciprocates Sai's movements without objection to his advances. As Sai sits, a human alongside another human, a man next to another man, the distance between their skins dissolves.

The boy seldom moves or withdraws. Sai holds his sitting posture to maximize the area of contact, occasionally withdrawing to prevent the boy from suspecting the obvious intention of his closeness.

An actor on stage announces in a loud voice,

"We that are true lovers run into strange capers."

Touch*

Sai always had an inkling about things being different for him, but he could never really pinpoint what that was exactly, or maybe he was just too embarrassed to accept it. Sai always believed such feelings for another man to be baseless and needed to be erased instantly. Sai in the past struggled considerably with these feelings but always found a way to crush them. But today, Sai has accepted his fate in silence. He no longer wants to protect himself from these thoughts that he formerly considered indulgent. The feeling was simply marvelous even though it was in conflict with what he had believed all his life. All through his twenty-five years of existence, he was incapable of expressing what he truly wanted. Anything outside of friendship with other men was out of the question for Sai. The boy was teaching him an important life lesson, about discovering your true self and the peculiarities of human nature. He felt he was being taken over by a force so strong and natural that it was impossible to deny to himself, his true self. Sai began to believe that anything might be possible.

Sai imagined the worst: if the boy were to figure out what was happening, Sai would be completely mortified. The boy probably would be steaming inside, but merely keep his cool, given his helplessness inside the confines of the packed theater. Sai prepares an imaginary rebuttal in his head in case he is confronted for his vile behavior. He would, pretend to be oblivious to the physical contact he had been forcing, claiming it was only accidental and not intentional.

While the play is well underway, Sai more than once glances in the boy's direction to sneak a peek at his face. The boy looks adorable, lovely, lovable, tempting, and cuddly – but uninterested.

The play marches on trying to win appreciation. The audience around Sai erupts into laughter and cheers. The dancing, screaming high-pitched dialogue does not seem to entertain much less distract Sai from the joy of the boy's touch.

Sai hopes there is an intermission so that he can strike up a conversation.

After an hour and a half, to Sai's horror, he realizes that to prevent distortion in the audience's train of thought, the director has decided to eliminate the intermission.

Touch*

It's a short play, soon to be over. The play is in Act V Scene 4, the protagonist on stage is weeping, and Sai probably has only another fifteen minutes left of this heavenly touch. His only wish is for time to stop.

Finally, the play ends. All the characters in the play make up for lost love or find new lovers. The play ends with a light-hearted message, which is, "In the realm of love, you can choose as you please." The actors take their bows and the spotlight retracts.

The lights inside the theater are raised. The faces in the audience now become visible. Before Sai can turn to see him one final time, the boy rises quickly and makes his way to the exit. Sai gets one final look at his back as the boy files out of the theater. Sai is hoping that at the very least, he could have said goodbye to the boy. The boy vanishes into thin air, however, and he is lost forever. Sai felt everything; the boy felt nothing. This was just an unnecessary interference to Sai's otherwise routine life, leaving Sai to face an inconvenient truth about himself.

As they walk away from the theater, Sai's girlfriend takes his arm and holds it tightly against her chest, asking him, "So - did you enjoy the pay? Were you able to follow? You seemed distracted throughout."

Sai looking straight into her eyes, says, "I did, I followed most of it."

Sai wonders if she had picked up on how he felt during the play. Her arm bothers Sai, a slight twitch conveys to her, his irritation and she withdraws it. Sai plunges both his hands in the front pocket of his jeans to keep them out of reach, and to control himself from using them otherwise.

Sai, tormented by the clash of his feelings, admonishes himself, *"This cannot be happening - what is wrong with me."*

His girlfriend angrily asks him, "What's the problem? Did I say something I should not have?"

Sai is forced to lie again, "Nothing I'm sorry - just have a lot on my mind at the moment."

His girlfriend, "I don't understand."

Sai clears his throat and mutters, "Forget about it, let's just go home."

Both walk silently side-by-side. Both have very different ideas as to what should happen next.

His girlfriend forcibly wraps her arm around his arm. She perhaps is trying to signal what should happen next. Sai in his distractive state appears even more charming. All she wants to do is pull him close and walk home arm in arm. His girlfriend mistakenly thinks the glow of adoration he is carrying on his face is for her.

But Sai will have none of that, all he can think about is the boy. It was no ordinary touch, it caused a latent desire, to unhinge itself and erupt into a nonsensical longing.

Sai with his fears quelled knows he is headed in a new direction, and soon will have to take to a new life as to the manner born.

"The show is over - 'And thereby hangs a tale.'"

Vanity

Louis is on the verge of calling it quits. He has been laboring over his novel for the last eleven years. He has painstakingly revised several drafts and fixed everything in the novel that required attention. He has even hired freelance editors and proofreaders to polish the content to make the text more readable and in turn, marketable.

Louis has sent out hundreds of book proposals, made several in-person book pitches, and submitted no less than four hundred and fifty query letters to literary agents. Not a single letter managed to grab the attention of the sharp editorial eyes, nor did a single editor request the manuscript.

The rejections came at an alarming pace from the gatekeepers of the publishing industry, mainly from publishers in the English-speaking worlds of North America and the UK. The consensus seemed to be that his novel lacked literary merit and did not meet their standards. The novel also did not fit into the trending genres of the given year - mind-body-spirit connection, magical realism, and dystopian young adult romance.

Louis' novel is a life saga. A long story of the heroic accomplishments of a young Muslim boy. Lacking trendy content it ends up in the slush pile of every publisher, by default. One London publisher sniffed, "that they publish only quality literature and he might have better luck with another publishing company in his home country, the USA."

And in the USA, a stylistic editor in New York, suggested Louis rewrite his novel to reduce the number of conflicts faced by the protagonist, to make it less confusing for the American reader. In the novel, the protagonist's heroism stems from his ability to overcome the never-ending stream of misfortunes in his life. Louis had masterfully and meticulously crafted and layered the protagonist's character so the suggestion to cutback puts him in absolute horror.

The frequency of the acrimonious rejections began to shatter Louis' belief in his ability to tell stories. The many disapprovals were like nails being driven into his literary coffin. He became filled with self-doubt.

Louis is in his mid-fifties. He has forfeited a well-paying, secure corporate job to pursue his passion: To make a living as a writer, a low-paying, high-effort, with an uncertain career path. To date, he has lived off his savings, compromised his lifestyle, and invested both - effort and money. He is determined to have his novel see the light of day. He is not ready to give in just yet.

So as an alternative strategy, he decides to market his book in different geographies. With what remained of his grit, he forwards the manuscripts to literary agents in Asia.

To his delight, he receives a response from an agent in India within a couple of days. The agent accepts his book *as-is* and within months the novel finds a home with a publishing house in New Delhi.

As the novel starts to hit bookstore shelves across India, Louis's life starts to change as sales numbers rise.

At the insistence of his publisher in India, Louis relocates from his home in Irvine, CA to Mumbai. He begins his first book tour in a foreign country. As part of the two-month-long book tour, Louis has to attend book launches at coffee shops, bookstores, and book fairs in big cities and smaller towns across the country. Louis begins to gain a wider audience for his novel with several press releases, back-page stories in the dailies, an interview on page six in the evening paper, and a minute-long radio spot on an early morning talk show, featuring sound bites from his novel.

Louis participates in several panel discussions at literary festivals. At these events, Louis makes it a point to sit on stage, with both hands holding the novel straight up over his right knee, with the cover facing the audience, for all to see. His publisher insists that he do so. After the discussions, he patiently waits in the book signing stalls. The stalls are stacked with piles of freshly-printed hard copies on the table, and on the back wall hangs a poster of

Quriously

the novel and a framed portrait of himself. Buyers of his novel stand in long queues in front of the table with a copy of the novel in their hands.

Louis sits at the edge of a foldable wooden chair behind the white-draped table, to graciously greet and personally autograph his novel for all of his avid readers.

He is a 'persona nongrata' in his home country, the US. The novel finds a home in a remote land and he is a celebrity there. For Louis, it is a blessing that his novel finally resonates with such a large audience, and his hard work is paying off.

In the second month after publication, the publisher authorizes a second, much larger print run. As the novel gains traction, the publisher advises Louis to start marketing the book aggressively and explore innovative ideas to enhance audience engagement.

His publisher says, "Explore all avenues and most importantly increase the footprint of your social media presence, create a buzz about your book - get people talking about it."

Though the push to market comes from the publisher, the publisher does little else to support sales. Louis must invest considerable sums of money to promote his book. After all, he wants to maintain the recent momentum in book sales. His ambition is to have his novel on the bestseller list.

Louis decides to capitalize on the recent attention his novel is drawing. He begins to organize book launches at local bookstores and community centers. At these events, he invites celebrities - actors and writers - to endorse the book and exchange kind words. He pays for cake and coffee and he distributes free t-shirts with the book cover printed on front.

Louis comes to understand the new paradigm in book-selling: even if a book finds a reputable publisher, the onus to sell largely rests with the author.

In addition to the conventional sales methods to attract new readers, Louis decides to become an active social media participant. Up until now, he has been dormant on Facebook, Twitter, and Instagram. He has accounts on all three but seldom logs in. With his growing popularity and his newfound excitement, the publisher's words ring true. Louis needs to shift his focus and hype himself up on social media sites.

On his road to glory, Louis, unfortunately, encounters many disappointments. He publishes parts of his novel on Medium, receives limited views and claps, and posts excerpts on Facebook, and the number of likes and followers is much below his expectations.

He assumes the social channels will cultivate a following and the followers he hopes will buy. He believes that sales are directly proportional to the number of followers. But he discovers that no matter how hard he tries, he never receives more than a few likes and only a handful of followers.

On several occasions, Louis is reminded by his publisher, "Every author who wants his literary career to head in a purposeful direction needs an audience. And, therefore it is mandatory that every author build a fanbase in today's digital age. Every author needs to adopt a serious social media strategy."

Being publish-worthy is a significant milestone for Louis. However, failing to grow his follower base, despite his efforts, Louis decides to inject life into his social media campaign. He hires the services of a professional social media consultant.

The consultant he hires calls herself Alexei. Alexei is recommended by a digital marketing agency called "Blue Lemonade," and on Instagram, her handle is "@sociallysavvy." Alexei's profile description is, "I help entrepreneurs unleash their inner STAR through engaging IG content."

Alexei is a chirpy twenty-something, with presumably incredible social media ability. At eighteen she dropped out of college and began a career as a digital marketer. Her hustle is to place relevant digital content on appropriate sites and locate the right audience for her clients.

The cafe's around the city serve as her office, and she needs nothing other than her iPhone and her MacBook Air to operate. She has been a game-changer for several Instagram startups. Her book of successes include:

"@Banggreat" a brand for male underwear which redefines masculinity;

"@Rainbowcakes" a favorite amongst hipsters;

"@ShihTzuPups" which grows to have a hundred thousand followers in a year;

"@ecocanyon" - a brand that promotes sustainable clothing to make people question what they wear or if they have too many clothes;

Her claim to fame is her ability to turn lackluster profiles into sought-after Instagram handles.

Alexei takes a first look at Louis' Instagram account, and concludes it is amateurish at best. Her comments are, "The style is inconsistent, there is no overarching theme. The pictures are sub-par, poorly staged, badly lit, and caption-less. "

Alexei tells Louis, "Starting today, be more particular when taking photos and archive all the existing poor-quality photos."

Louis guesses she means to say, "Delete everything on the current page ASAP."

Alexei adds, "It is no secret that posts with captions attract more engagement than those without."

Alexei emphasizes using relevant hashtags, a maximum of five with each post.

She offers several other pieces of advice to Louis on how to create a stronger presence online and how to *project* himself.

She advises him to, "Start doing it right and improve his Instagram aesthetic to increase the number of followers."

Louis' Instagram account has been used primarily to archive pictures from his childhood and school days. On one unfortunate day, his iMac had crashed, and with that crash, all of his cherished photographs vanished into thin air - photographs of him spending time with his father in his last days, of working in Luxembourg in his twenties, and of his wedding. The wedding had been over for ten years, the pictures remained a sour reminder of the bitter divorce. Louis still hung on to them for years, but on the day of the hard-disk crash, he felt no loss.

Louis had gone through life, replacing laptops every two to three years. Each new laptop required the tedious job of backing up and restoring the pictures. To make this effort more efficient he decided to archive the pictures on an internet cloud rather than on the laptops' hard drives.

Louis had chosen Instagram for the application's ease of use. In the beginning, he was unnerved by the fact that the entire world was privy to the photographs of his life. However, to salvage his memories for the future, the benefits seemed to outweigh the lack of privacy, and he started to use Instagram on a limited need-to-store basis.

After three years of existence on Instagram, most of his fifty followers were family and friends. Being shy and introverted he infrequently took pictures of himself and rarely uploaded them.

When he did post, it was pictures of sunrises or monuments, never of himself. He never used the story feature, reels, or the highlight feature which combined several multiple stories on his profile page. Using the features built into the Instagram camera like *boomerang* and *superzoom* was entirely out of the question!

Alexie knows she has to change Louis' thinking. So she asks him, to promote on his Instagram wall with pictures of a fun and vibrant lifestyle. "Get interactive, tag and comment, acknowledge your audience," she said, "Start using Instagram stories. Collaborate extensively, and endorse meaningful partnerships with writers, designers, musicians, artists, and photographers. Mail copies of your book to book bloggers and meme influencers, and tease content to lead the audience to a purchase link of the book. Tailor content that grabs attention and speaks to all generations - from sluggish gen-Xers to the quick millennials."

Louis concludes that Alexei's suggestions meant one thing and one thing alone: that he will now have to take a lot of captivating images and videos of himself.

She unabashedly reminds him on several occasions that he should keep the focus on himself.

She says, "Try and post as many pictures of yourself alone as you can. Look at any celebrity's Instagram wall - they only have pictures of themselves. That is why it is called a vanity wall."

Louis is self-conscious and has been living invisibly all his life. He is someone to whom even making small talk seems like a burden. The act of taking endless pictures of himself, repeatedly, seems like a daunting task. Excessive pride and focus on one's work or one's self seem arrogant, ostentatious, narcissistic, conceited, and, to say the very least, affected.

Now, with his book gaining traction, however, he knows he must boost his Instagram account and make its content seductive so that he can attract more followers. "For what is an author who has no readers, no audience?" he hears Alexei's voice in his head.

As Louis browses through several profiles on Instagram, he starts to believe Instagram is crowded with selfie-obsessed players. All the accounts that Alexei has asked him to review are of much younger authors, bonafide influencers, legit bloggers, genuine trailblazers, unquestionable style consultants, and celebutantes. Most are millennials who are just starting their careers and are full of optimism and youthful beauty. They look striking in every picture from every angle and in every light, their facial complexion bursting with elastin.

The posters are all selfie-kings and selfie-queens, who with careful staging and color-correction, make themselves look great in every post. Youth is a synonym for beauty!

Louis thinks if you're a millennial, you love your selfies. If you are over a certain age, say fifty you hate them. This is perhaps the new generational divide.

Louis wonders if they are hiding a secret. When he asks Alexei about all of this, she reveals the secret is to practice. She says, "With practice, every selfie, every post, can be fabulously alluring."

How can Louis compete with this? So, he begins to practice, practice, practice. Having taken hundreds of pictures of himself, he scrutinizes every picture for hours until he figures out which are the perfect pictures of his face, the perfect pose, the perfect look. He realizes a selfie is about creating and constructing an illusion.

Louis poses for each selfie and more often than not he takes one look, grunts, and instantly deletes it. He repeats the process several times, but the outcome is always below the mental image he has of his good looks. There's no escaping the passage of time – you get older and your body ages. He has creases on his face, sleep wrinkles, and the daily stress that makes his face look puffy. No matter from which angle he takes his selfie, his face always looks distorted.

He tries holding the camera up and then down. He holds his chin up and then down. He tries smiling, then looking grim but nothing works. His face looks tired, and the expression in his eyes always comes across as bitter. In images with heavy-duty editing, he transforms into someone, who even he does not recognize. The software can make him young in the face but he remains susceptible to the signs of aging in the other parts of his body. He feels particularly old in the knees.

Louis is officially now in narcissistic hell, one for which even Dante has no circle. He thinks narcissism is now not only acceptable, but it's also expected. Louis can guess what Alexei will say: "Selfies are a way to show self-love rather than a form of narcissism."

Louis, much against his will, goes on a blitzkrieg to fertilize his Instagram page, he takes pictures every day, everywhere, with everyone - in the hope to become Instafamous one day. He assumes that taking and posting pictures of himself will be pivotal to an effective marketing strategy.

He posts curated pictures from every book launch, and book signing and from moments when he fulfills selfie requests made by fans and volunteers. He posts pictures of himself highlighting his progress in fitness, his environmentally conscious vegan diet, gourmet kale salads, beetroot-detox smoothies, and other trivialities of his daily life. He hashtags such photos as #candid. On rare occasions, he posts panoramic shots of himself with beautiful landscapes in the backdrop, and on other occasions, he superimposes inspirational quotes on his portrait. He packages and distributes every photo, whether it comes out of his morning run or while cooking his meals.

He updates selfies on Instagram stories several times a day, every hour in fact, as he goes about the minutiae of his suddenly peachy life, from the moment he wakes up to the moment he goes to bed.

He uses hashtags, geotags, emojis, and the new age (clever to practical) acronyms - irl, lol, lmao, qq, tmi. He discovers that acronyms require less thumb work than whole words and it also feels good using them. He at last feels like he is finally in the know.

He adopts all the social media trends, and posts forwards related to reading, writing, books, and literature. He follows the Instagram handles of prominent authors and book clubs in various parts of the country and the world. He stalks book clubs sponsored by Bollywood stars of yesteryear and pays close attention to what the stars are currently reading, watching, and promoting. He likes and acknowledges the handful of comments he receives on his posts and makes it a point to comment back to show that he cares. He updates his profile picture every week.

With every post, he takes stock of the number of likes and comments he has, and any new followers that have been added. As the months go by, the results of his efforts start to unfold. His life is hardly as glamorous as those of the influencers he follows. He lacks an awesome sports car or cool sunglasses. Suddenly he begins to suffer lifestyle envy. He starts feeling deprived. No matter how hard he tries to make his content engaging or to promote himself or his book on social media, the likes are few, and the followers even fewer. Something is not working. He starts to accept the fact that his life is not Instagrammable. He hoped to be showered with attention and when that does not happen, it starts to gnaw at his self-esteem and slowly fills him with a feeling of inadequacy.

For his poor showing in follower growth after four months, - Alexei tells him, "Patience is key. More often than not, you will not be able to see outstanding results overnight."

She barrels on, "Focus on your vanity metrics - likes, comments, and followers. Remix it, maybe this time with an ad campaign for a specific demographic. When you target audiences, carefully consider their psychographics, their interests and their attitudes. Use guerrilla marketing strategies and see how that works. Most influencers rely on their *follower and like counts for business*."

Louis politely listens to her but internally starts to resent her. Being told by a twenty-something what to do and how to do it is grating.

However, to accommodate her suggestions, Louis has developed a standard response that ends with him saying, "You know what? You're right. I'll change right away!"

But as he says that, this time, it does not feel right. This time he begins to second-guess himself. He does not want to fall prey to the trappings of social media and decides to step back his forays into that world. Having spent endless amounts of time on social media activities, he has begun to engage less and less in face-to-face relationships. He has also reduced his investment in other meaningful activities. He has become sedentary and has sent the weekly screen time spent on his phone through the roof.

He self-diagnoses, deciding that the preoccupation with himself is a risky behavior pattern to maintain. The more time he spends on social media, the lonelier and more anxious he feels. He becomes superficial and shallow without any real substance. If he continues on his current path he knows his mental issues will be exacerbated and will eventually drive him into depression and psychologically distressing states.

He has become mentally simple, spending a lot of time clicking through pictures of himself and of others while waiting all the time for something to happen. Instagram makes him feel like a liar and manipulator. He finds the social media space confusing and starts to become defensive and angry.

Just as any self-respecting author worth his salt will feel, Louis starts to doubt the usefulness of his effort on social sites. He feels the amount of time he spends on social media, could be better spent on writing his next novel. Not being successful on Instagram is making him feel like a failure, which he knows he is not.

He has felt proud of being able to sell more than five thousand copies of his book through conventional sales channels. On the other hand, Instagram has neither provided significant sales nor any meaningful business relationships.

At fifty, Louis turns into a cynic, censor, and critic of the usefulness of Instagram. Instagram spins him on all his twelve axes like twisting a Rubik's cube. The platform is forcing him to hold an unrealistically superior view of himself. All his life he has been reclusive and an over-thinker. Falling prey to the carrot of Instagram, he has done the unthinkable, he has tried to become an upbeat extrovert and non-thinker, simply for the sake of others.

Louis decides he is returning to his old understated way of hiding behind the scenes, convinced that he had been given the wrong advice by Alexei. Creating a vanity wall was simply not well suited to his personality. The next day he calls Alexei and tells her in a rather presidential tone - "You are fired!"

Louis wonders aloud to himself as he reflects on the past few months *"That was dumb - human folly outdoing itself - but yes there were more than a few laughs on this wild ride!"*

"Mubarak"

Muzamil, Mubarak, Mehtaab, Mehmet are all names with sounds that roll off the tongue in a calming, melodic way. They taste sweet, smooth, and velvety like wine rolling around the tongue. Euphonious like a rushing stream, evoking the image of an open field. Trevor self-indulgently says them, drops them, and uses them as often as he can.

Trevor thinks he has always had an attraction to names of Arabic or Farsi origin. Unlike the Christian names he is used to, they tickle his soul.

His personal favorite is the name, *Mubarak*. The name can have several meanings depending on its usage. It can mean commendation, blessing, grace, or benediction, and generally is used as a suffix for birthdays, weddings, or celebrations. "Janm-Din-

Mubarak" for example means happy birthday, and "Shaadi Mubarak" means congratulations on your wedding.

Mubarak, the name, has an Arabic origin and is analogous to the Hebrew name *Barak* derived from Semitic roots. Mubarak is also a Sikh name. Several Sikhs from the state of Punjab in India often name their children using names of Arabic or Persian origin.

The tenth Guru of the Sikhs, a Persian scholar, for both of his sons, used names of Arabic origin *Fateh Singh* and *Zorawar Singh*.

The Sikh scriptures contain lots of Persian words. The Gurbani (the holy scripture of the Sikhs) uses several words of Arabic origin, like *Raheem* (merciful), *Kareem* (benevolent), *Fateh* (victory), and *Tanveer* (beautiful). All are beautiful names generally assumed to be Arabic but also common amongst the Sikhs. Such names usually are a testament to the contradiction between their heritage and perception.

To finally have a friend named *Mubarak* meant the world to Trevor. Everyone he believed should have at least one friend with an Arabic name. Trevor's friend, Mubarak is a recent import into Mumbai from a farming village in Punjab. He arrived, looking for his big break into the worlds of fashion, television, and movies, not necessarily in that order.

And as Mubarak waits, he has turned himself into a gym-honed Adonis. Pre-Workouts nourish his bronzed musculature. Obsessive doses of BCA's and whey protein shakes have led to lean, vascular muscles on his biceps, triceps, pecs, and hamstrings. He dresses in tank tops and knee-high board shorts, clothes that reveal his sensual arms and alluring legs. A fine specimen of good health - running, swimming, skipping, and gymming every day, twice a day. His optimism is evident in his vibrant brown eyes, believing the day is not far off when his dream will unfold - his image on the cover of Cosmopolitan or Stardust, after amassing over a million Instagram followers.

Trevor is from southern California and is on sabbatical in India. His business school study group partner, Arun, had recently moved to India to start a tech company. With a failed business and

"Mubarak"

bankruptcy, and facing unaffordable healthcare in America, Trevor had agreed to relocate to India for a year, upon Arun's recommendation, Trevor decided to partner with Arun on a new tech venture to get his life back on track.

India has been welcoming and friendly and Trevor has found it to be a good place to regroup and rewire. By virtue of his pale skin, he enjoys star-like status in the country and is treated like royalty.

Trevor met Mubarak in a local gym. Alternating sets of tricep pushdowns and small talk after reps, the casual acquaintance blossomed into a friendship. Mubarak, as it happens, lives down the street from Trevor in a one-room studio. Trevor finds Mubarak easy to like and, on most days, they get along. Physical proximity helps them share the routines of life. They go for runs in the parks, for quick bites, and for long drives. For Trevor, a local friend assuages life's inconveniences that stem from a lack of time or a social network. Whether it is procuring medications, picking up a serviced car, or assembling furniture, Mubarak is always willing to help.

Mubarak is calm and compassionate but always late — a millennial side-effect. Every movie night begins with Trevor arriving early, waiting, and pacing. Eventually, Mubarak usually arrives, offering a smile and assurance that they will still make the show on time.

Mubarak is also somewhat naive. Trevor blames the twenty-five years of his life, that he has lived so far. He bets with Trevor that Toronto is the capital of Canada, and loses. Then he bets on Trump defeating Clinton in the US Presidential race this time, and to Trevor's surprise, Mubarak wins. Mubarak in his naivete, believes that studying the odds and high-stakes betting on premier league cricket matches is an easy way to make a quick buck.

Mubarak's full-time job, while he is waiting for his career to turn around, is a dating app, on which he has no qualms of spending countless hours a day.

One day, while helping Trevor restore data from an old computer, he comes across an archive of Trevor's pictures in a folder called Travel. As they start to browse through pictures of Trevor's past life, Mubarak enthusiastically enquires about the places in the pictures. The bluffs along the Pacific coast highway, the painted deserts of the Grand Canyon, the General Sherman sequoia in Yosemite, and the Bermuda beaches, all pique his curiosity. Trevor concludes that Mubarak is eager to embark on new adventures and visit new places.

Mubarak is much younger than Trevor, who has befriended Mubarak not because they have a lot in common, but because he lives nearby, and has a name that he is enchanted by. Trevor uses the name in conversations more than is necessary. Mubarak becomes the preferred name to use with baristas, concierges, receptionists, front desks, valets, and other gatekeepers. It is the name given when coffee is to be picked up, a dinner reservation is made, or the car is parked.

In the summer of 2018, Trevor informs Mubarak about his plans to visit Israel. Being well aware of Mubarak's interest in visiting new places, Trevor asks him if he would like to join.

"I am going on a ten-day trip to the holy land of Israel - wanna come?" he casually asks.

Mubarak replies, "I don't know much about Israel, but I have a friend who went to Jordan and he loved it."

Trevor - "Jordan is across the dead sea from Israel, the two countries are neighbors," Trevor says.

"Jordan may be a better destination," Mubarak concludes.

The two friends initially debate the charms of each country. Both have bewitching desert scenery, magical wadi's, and buoyant dead sea floatation. Jordan has Amman, the world heritage site in Petra, and no Visa requirement for an Indian national.

Israel has the vibrant Mediterranean beaches of Tel Aviv and abundant historic sites - the Western Wall, the Church of the Holy Sepulchre, and the fascinating cities of Jerusalem, Haifa, and Jericho. But Israel also has rigorous Visa requirements.

To choose between the two, one of them has to decide, and the other has to agree. Trevor picks Israel and Mubarak picks Jordan. The decision is made in Trevor's favor by Mubarak's father, an orange plantation owner in northwest Punjab. The father, whom Trevor has never met in person, secretly hopes that Mubarak, his only son, will forego his Bollywood dreams and return to Punjab to contribute to the generations-old family farming business.

The father advises Mubarak to go to the young country of Israel. "Israel," the father says, "has found miraculous ways since the 1950s to green their desert. The Israelis have made significant breakthroughs in farming techniques such as drip irrigation to conserve water, the use of natural pesticides, and grain cocoons."

What cinches the deal is that Trevor assures Mubarak that he will have no difficulty procuring a Visa for Israel, with an American co-traveller. After all, Israel is another one of the states of the U.S.

To please his father and somewhat convinced by Trevor's argument, Mubarak agrees to a trip to Israel. As they plan their journey, the two friends set their sights on the beaches and the monuments of Israel. To make the trip purposeful, as advised by his father, they plan on visiting a couple of kibbutzim to learn Israeli farming techniques. At last, the dream of a fun summer romp in the merciless sun of the Israeli summer begins to materialize.

From this point forward, a strange coincidence starts to occur. Visit Israel, themed commercials begin to appear on several TV channels. The Israeli Ministry of Tourism has spent millions on a summer campaign to lure Indians to visit Israel during the peak holiday season, May and June. Going by the frequency of television commercials showcasing the beauty and diversity of the country, the friends assume the Israeli Department of Tourism is extending a personal invitation to them. Hopefully, the Department will also streamline the entry and exit requirements for Indian tourists. Little do they know that they are stepping into the crosshairs of Israeli paranoia!

Procuring a visa in Mumbai for Mubarak, the holder of an Indian passport, requires three trips to the Israeli embassy. Mubarak has to present extensive documentation related to work and income history. Two rounds of interviews seem excessive, but in the end, seal the deal.

"*Mubarak*"

Once Mubarak has successfully obtained a Visa, they take a celebratory drive across Malabar Hill and stop to take a picture on a hilltop with the clear blue skies of Marine Drive in the backdrop. With arms across each other's shoulders, they ask a passer-by for the click. The picture is the first of many such images that will soon follow from the upcoming vacation.

When the day of departure finally arrives, El Al, Israel's national air carrier, instructs them to arrive four hours before departure, to allow sufficient time for check-in. Trevor had chosen the carrier El Al so they could have an immersive Israeli experience enroute. He hopes flight announcements will be in Hebrew and they will be able to sample kosher cuisine onboard. For Trevor, El Al is the first testament to the very existence of Israel.

Trevor hopes for the usual when they arrive at the Mumbai airport: stand in queue for the boarding passes, drop the bags, grab a drink, and head to the gate for take-off.

However, this is not to be. When they step up to the flight counter, they are asked to wait in a cordoned-off section outside the check-in desks. The security staff attends to them individually, perpetually skeptical, security agents and airline staff members go back and forth discussing the various findings. They keep the passengers under their fixed gaze, studying every move, tracking every movement - taking unprecedented amounts of time. Trevor and Mubarak begin to wonder if they will be cleared to board the flight. Is this uncertainty a security tactic to reveal a passenger's bad intentions?

Two nuns, referred to as sisters in India, wait patiently in line behind them. One of them notices the friends' discomfort and assures them that this is routine. They tell Trevor this happens every time they fly, which they have been doing for the last seven years.

Finally, it is Trevor's turn, to answer a series of questions (similar to the ones he answered during his interview at the embassy). He provides the paperwork for a reexamination:

"Which school did you go to?"

"Who bought your ticket?"

"Do you have a credit card?"

"Do you have enough money?"

"Why do you want to go to Tel Aviv?"

"Where will you stay?"

"Have you been to any Arab country?"

Trevor wonders what the security team is trying to establish as the agents barrage them with questions.

The agents strip Trevor and Mubarak of their life stories, work histories, income details, and family backgrounds. The stringent security measures leave less than a shining first impression of Israelis.

After all the questions and answers are complete, they are allowed to drop the bags, in exchange for boarding passes, and proceed to the departure gate. There is no time left for a drink or a snack. As they enter the aircraft, the flight attendant greets them with a "Shalom." The greeting instantly reminds Trevor of all those Visit Israel TV commercials, warmly inviting them to the country.

An image flashes across Trevor's mind of all the Israeli tourists that come to Goa's beaches and flood the Manali hills during breaks that follow the compulsory military training in Israel. Trevor thinks to himself, "Does the Indian Department of Tourism subject all Israeli visitors to a similar level of scrutiny at check-in?"

As they take to the skies, Trevor realizes that the flight takes a circuitous route after take-off from Mumbai. It first flies west over the Arabian Sea to the horn of Africa, and then north over the Red Sea into Israel, avoiding the airspaces of several Islamic countries. What could have been a five-hour flight (if flown as a crow flies) turned into an eight-hour flight due to the route blocks imposed by Israel's Arab neighbors. Upon touchdown, they disembark from the airbridge and follow the immigration signs in the long white corridors of Tel Aviv's Ben Gurion airport. Trevor can't help but notice the stark and solemn nature of the airport: grey walls with minimal advertising all in need of a facelift.

There are men in uniform everywhere. Trevor and Mubarak approach passport control and stand in the shortest line. They are immediately stopped by an armed, uniformed soldier who tells them that the line is for Israeli citizens only. He asks them to move to a much longer line.

It is finally their turn for the arrival interview.

The interaction with the immigration officer is quick. He studies and stamps their papers. His hollow eyes take one look at Mubarak's passport, and he is instantly aggravated. Incensed, with the passport in hand, he leaves his cubicle. He returns with an officer who immediately asks both Trevor and Mubarak to follow him to a holding area.

Trevor and Mubarak trundle their luggage and are made to sit on the grey stainless-steel benches of a windowless holding room to wait for clearance. From the moment Trevor sits down, he notices something the other travellers in that room have in common. Everyone in the room, besides himself, is non-Caucasian and most likely non-Jewish either Black, Asian, Latino, or Arab. Trevor begins feeling anxious.

An immigration officer appearing to be of a higher rank greets Trevor and Mubarak with an indecipherable frown. He clears Trevor due to his American passport and then asks both of them to follow him into an office, situated on the left of the holding area. The little room looks like an interrogation room. The walls of the room are bare, and the paint is stripping at the corners, no flag of Israel, no star of David, no picture of its great leaders. Simple - only a painted wooden desk and three wooden chairs. The furniture is rundown and in need of a fresh coat of varnish. An air of seriousness fills the room. All of Trevor's excitement about being in Israel is overshadowed by an uneasy sense of foreboding.

The officer wearing a suspicious gaze shuts the door and sits on the table with Mubarak's passport in hand, leafing through it. Both friends nervously await another round of invasive questioning.

The officer asks Mubarak between long and deep silences, "How long will you stay in Israel?" "Do you have other forms of Identification?" "Do you speak Hebrew or Arabic?"

And so on - pausing, observing, staring.

Minutes begin to tick by like hours. Trevor senses Mubarak is getting tired and starting to feel drained. However, Mubarak continues to stand in silent acquiescence to all the prodding. He digs deep to muster up the resilience to battle this interrogation.

With the next question, the security officer thinks he has hit the jackpot. He asks Mubarak, "So what are you? are you Moslem? Because Mubarak is an Arabic name"

Mubarak replies, "No I am Hindu"

The interrogating officer, "Are you from Pakistan?"

Mubarak, taken aback by the illogical assumption, "I was born in India in Punjab."

The interrogating officer mispronounces and asks to confirm, "Poonjaab?"

Mubarak, "Yes, it is a state in India, in northern India, and shares its western border with Pakistan"

The officer now visibly displeased, "So do you feel more Indian or Pakistani - surely, with a name like Mubarak you must feel more Moslem"

Mubarak tries to convince the officer stating that he has never been out of India and this is his first trip. The officer asks him about the nature of his visit and if he plans to visit the West Bank. Mubarak responds by saying, "I am only accompanying my friend

Trevor who is an American citizen for a week's vacation." By the expression on the security officer's face, it seems like he does not like Mubarak's answer, and he repeatedly insists that Mubarak is an Arabic name and he should not lie to him. To Mubarak, it feels like the officer cannot get enough of mocking and humiliating him.

Mubarak feels the punch of the accusation, like an arrow going through his heart. He does his best to explain honestly, that he is from Punjab. Many Hindus mainly Sikhs, in Punjab use Arabic and Farsi names, as has been the tradition for centuries. The Officer looks displeased and without a response leaves the detention room, most likely to validate what Mubarak has just tried to explain to him.

Trevor wonders why Mubarak must explain this to a prejudiced Israeli officer. He has a *VISA* issued by the Israeli embassy. Why is the name so disarming for the officer? Why does a mellifluous name such as *Mubarak* spell so much trouble? If this were to turn out badly for Mubarak, Trevor would regret picking Israel over Jordan.

The long flight, waiting in queues, and lack of an early morning coffee are beginning to take a toll on both of them. Trevor feels drained, and witnessing his friend being treated like a criminal is making him furious. Trevor is teetering on a meltdown. He wonders why the security officer left the room and what possible outcome could he come back with. Is there a system in the backroom that can cross-check to see if Mubarak is telling the truth? Trevor wants to aid his friend, and he decides that when the officer returns, he will tell him, "Plug *Mubarak* into a search engine or query some secret global database. You will discover Mubarak is clean and has no prior criminal history." Trevor is nervous that the officer will make a decision detrimental to their upcoming trip, with limited information and based on his quick and incorrect judgment of Mubarak's name.

Trevor begins to wonder if Israel's attempts to portray itself as a vibrant, liberal country that promotes pluralism and diversity and advocates inclusiveness holds any truth. What right does the Officer have to treat people with such impunity?

What kind of suspicion can a name arouse? Perhaps it arouses suspicion of one's association with a terrorist group or with the convoluted world of espionage - based on the fact that his name sounds, Arabic.

The security officer returns. He frowns and asks Mubarak for his phone. He looks at the phone and frowns deeper, as though the phone has let him down. His frown switches to a snicker and he asks Mubarak, "So if I scan your phone, I will not find anything anti-Israeli, will I?" Before Mubarak can say "No" to such a baseless question, the officer returns the passport to Mubarak and exits the room. Trevor is glad that the officer found nothing and has cleared them to leave. Maybe this is a customary welcome to a tourist in Israel. What did the officer fear that Mubarak was anti-semitic because of his name?

Trevor notices that their passports do not bear a stamp, only an Israeli entry card, which has been inserted between the visa pages. Trevor leaves the room thinking that this tiny country, with many enemies, maybe the reason for requiring such strenuous security checks. It is holy land where much blood has been spilled for centuries. Where hostility of the past resurfaces in the present. Jews were subject to persecution for their names for centuries, now it seems like they are justifying a policy of crucifying (metaphorically) people based on their names.

After they pick up their bags from the conveyor belts, they head to the parking lot where their rental car is ready for the taking. As they enter the car park, Trevor notices the light in this place is striking! He feels radiant, finding the land to have an unearthly beauty! Maybe it's the lingering spirit of Jesus!

Trevor and Mubarak turn on the engine and drive into the plentiful sunshine on Tel Avis's highways.

?Answer

The Japanese have a simple expression, 'mizo no kokoro' which means the 'mind is like water.' It flows reflects, and adapts.

Yuki wants his mind to be like the still waters of a pond, void of all ripples. In his mid-forties, he decides to leave Tokyo, to seek nomadic solitude. So, he sets out on a journey to a place where he might rid himself of fatigue from the monotony of his daily life. For most of the past fifteen years, Yuki has been married to a French woman. Eventually, cultural differences began to surface, and they soon felt like *gaijins* in each other's eyes, whether they were in Paris or Tokyo. After their split. Yuki begins to feel betrayed, cheated, and abandoned by those who were dearest to him.

Pondicherry is set in the southern state of Tamil Nadu and is so far from Tokyo that there are no physical reminders of his failed marriage. Yuki's thoughts are uncontrollable as he travels to India. His good and bad feelings churn endlessly. He suffers from futile and obsessive thinking. Yuki hopes the starkly different culture, the spicy food, and the hot balmy weather of Pondicherry will offer the necessary energy to renew his inner self.

It is Yuki's first trip to southern India. From the Chennai airport, Pondicherry is three hours by car. The East Coast Road is two-lane and narrow, with plenty of blind corners. One is at the mercy of rashly driven buses and a melee of two-wheelers. Free-willed pedestrians, goats, and cows crisscross the road from all directions without warning.

The road winds along the Bay of Bengal, offering views of white sandy beaches on the western side of the road and glimpses of backwaters glistening in the bright sun on the eastern side. Forts in ruin, architecturally marvelous catholic churches, and pious temples dedicated to Durga and Shiva dot the surrounding lush, green tropical forest.

Feisty fisherwomen line the sidewalks of the maritime fishing hamlets, trading the fresh catch of the day. The crimson-gilled fish decked with sand grains. The relentless hardworking fishermen work together to dry the abundant fish and mend their nets outside their closely packed brick houses with thatched roofs.

The road is flanked on both sides by a multitude of mangrove forests. The coconut palms reach for the blue skies and banyan, tamarind, and mango trees spice up the salty sea air.

The coastal seascape makes Yuki feel optimistic. He enjoys the sights as the cab driver snakes his way over the roads.

Yuki reaches Pondicherry without a single break, a supposedly three-hour-long journey that ends up taking five hours.

On the first day in the sleepy beach town of Pondicherry, Yuki settles into his hotel in the French Quarter, called White Town. He strolls through the leafy cobbled streets lined with French colonial-era villas and dotted with craft shops and quirky eateries.

Most streets have French names on blue-enamelled signposts. The two main thoroughfares through White Town are Rue Dumas and Rue Romain Rolland. His hotel is on Rue Romain, a street that like other streets in White Town has the villas painted in shell-white, vivid canary yellow, and other vibrant colors. The facades of the villas have tall, wooden window shutters, mostly double-hung and freshly painted in sea blues and verdant greens. The homeowners' dynamic exterior color choices reflect the joy they seek from personalization, the sight of which must make their hearts sing.

For lunch, Yuki experiments with Franco-Tamil cuisine, Authentic French dishes cooked with Indian spices. But in the end, the southern Indian spices always seem to overpower the preparation. Yuki finds dining in White Town a one-of-a-kind experience. An experience similar to Yuki's marriage which had been a mutually respectful experiment in the food and culture of the world's two gastronomic leaders.

Yuki discovers the street bazaars along Rue Suffren and boutique shops with attached cafes along Rue du Bazaar St Laurent. They have plenty of eco-friendly incense sticks, organic soaps, and handmade silks.

At the Aurobindo Ashram store, he is persuaded to purchase the synergy, spring-blossom perfume oil to smell clean, and the aloe vera gel for flawless skin. The vendors are warm and honest.

In the evening, Yuki walks along the boardwalk to enjoy the sunset at promenade beach. He feels Pondicherry's serenity and moves at a relaxed pace. He feels fresh.

The next day Yuki rents a motorized two-wheeler to visit Auroville, the *City of Dawn*, a town ten kilometres north of White Town.

The main purpose of his journey to Auroville is the 'Maitri Mandir' (the mind temple). Yuki's wife had worked there as a volunteer in her teen years and had always talked about going back. She had claimed it was the best place to farm and meditate and hopefully dreamed of retiring there to run a Franco-Japanese cafe. When Yuki arrived at the Auroville visitor center he was told the temple is closed on Tuesdays. However, if he chose to, he could view the temple from a distance, from the visitors' observation deck.

The deck is a ten-minute walk from the visitor center along a tree-lined path that makes Yuki feel like he is walking through a forest. The trail through the dense tropical underbrush passes over red Tamil soil. Several stone tablets are embedded in the ground along the path. Each tablet has a painting of a flower, with the flower's spiritual significance written below. Yuki notices the tablet with the white gladiolus spike with its sword-shaped leaves. The tablet's creator believed that the flower signifies receptivity - and had inscribed the following on the stone, 'Flowers are very receptive, and they are happy when they are loved.' Yuki has no reason to disagree, so he accepts the evaluation.

Yuki continues to the trail.

The day is overcast, and the drizzle has transformed the oppressive heat of the Coromandel Coast into a pleasantly cool early morning.

Raindrops linger on wildflowers and the leaves of trees, and Yuki welcomes them on his face.

The forest has a matrix of various tree species, shrubs, and lianas. Beyond the path, it is filled with palm trees, neem, cashew, and plenty of thorny bushes. The mango and jackfruit trees dot the vast expanse of red earth that has been carved by a labyrinth of gullies and ravines. There is no one else on the path but Yuki. The path has turned into a place of pleasant solitude. The surrounding forest is silent.

Before Yuki reaches the observation deck, the rain picks up speed, and he has to seek cover under a colossal banyan tree. The tree sits in the center of an open space with several of its large roots hanging from its oversized branches reaching to the ground below. The roots are trunk-like branches that expand the footprint of the tree. The size of the tree is splendid.

It is a five-minute walk from the banyan tree to the observation deck. When Yuki reaches the deck he notices that the Mind Temple is still a few hundred feet away. It is the closest that one is allowed to get to the sacred site.

From this distance, the temple looks like a secret retreat. It is designed to be a hermitage for those seeking answers and a hideaway for those facing difficult life questions. It stands in the middle of a well-manicured park. It has a shape similar to a giant globe, like a spaceship with golden scales.

Its man-made nature appears to be out of place with its natural surroundings. It is distant, unreachable, and seems cordoned off.

Then Yuki begins to observe closely. The longer he looks at it - the temple starts to open up like a flower first touched by sunlight, blossoming in the bright rays. The oversized, golden bulb has a distended ovule in its center. Twelve concrete petals are spread around its perimeter. The temple boldly withstands the strong gushes of winds around it and basks under the rays of the sun.

The longer he looks at it, the more it begins to reveal itself. The entire outer surface of the structure has a remarkable aesthetic. Convex and concave discs cover it completely. Its form and color, and perhaps its purpose are perfection. The years of painstaking labor and the indomitable spirit of the people who built it become evident. It's an endeavor of exquisite artistry. By any measure, Yuki had not anticipated the impact it would have on him at first sight.

Yuki is not satisfied viewing the temple from far away. The structure seems protected as if, perhaps it safeguards a treasure. He needs to figure out what that treasure is. He must return to view it up close. It would be criminal to not visit the temple from the inside. Yuki returns to the visitor center to book an inside tour of the temple for the following day.

Getting to the temple from his hotel is a one-hour ride on a two-wheeler. It is a bumpy ride on a noisy, potholed road with countless speed bumps. His painful lower back does not deter him. Yuki makes the trip as he is determined to discover the secret the temple holds.

When he finally arrives at Auroville on the following day, Yuki boards a bus with several other curious visitors, and they are driven toward the temple.

Upon reaching the entrance, several signs greet him: 'Photography not allowed.' 'No cameras, cell phones, bags, or water bottles.' All are required to deposit personal possessions in lockers before entering the park surrounding the temple.

A group of about twenty men and women have come to visit the temple on this day. An older American lady is their escort. Her name is Janice, and she has been living in Auroville for the last fifteen years. Her skin is freckled and tanned and there is a frankness about her, as there is about most Americans. She insists on undivided attention, demands total focus, and then recites the only mandatory mantra that must be practiced in the park, the mantra is 'clean, clean, clean.'

The park around the mandir is called the 'Park of Unity.' It has twelve small gardens, each adjacent to the twelve concrete petals that surround the central globe of the temple, making the whole park look like a lotus. Each garden has a name, and the name is a spiritual notion, such as Existence, Consciousness, Bliss, Light, Life, Power, Wealth, Utility, Progress, Youth, Harmony, and Perfection. Each concrete petal doubles as a meditation chamber on the inside and also has a moral value associated with it. The names are Aspiration, Sincerity, Humility, Gratitude, Perseverance, Receptivity, Progress,

Courage, Goodness, Generosity, Equality, and Peace.

Yuki feels elated as he is made to proceed toward the temple. He is asked to remove his shoes outside the meditation chambers and then is required to sit around a lotus pond. A waterfall passes through the carved petals, and he is made to meditate there for five minutes, being reminded constantly to stay quiet by the temple caretakers. The caretakers are middle-aged men and women, mostly European and American and a few of other unrecognizable nationalities, dressed similarly in soothing organic homespun cotton in pastel shades. Their expressions are kind and welcoming. The caretakers stand around the visitors with their heads and bodies bent forward, permanently in a bow position. The caretakers continually remind everyone to be quiet. They reprimand with a shush, or by placing the pointer finger on their lips at the slightest sound.

Participating in the very first exercise in meditation at the lotus waterfall begins to settle his mind. The weight of his thoughts starts to lift. Yuki begins to feel lighter. As he proceeds to enter the temple, he begins to sense its influence.

Inside the central dome of the temple, it is dark and mostly hollow; the floors have white carpeting, and the walls are grey industrial concrete. The hollow space of the sphere is cut in half by an imaginary horizontal plane, into two functional areas. The lower half is void, a space with nothing other than the elliptical ramps that rise circularly along its perimeter. The ramps, with their gentle slope, lead you to the upper half of the dome. There are no windows. The top half is the inner chamber or a meditation chamber which is the heart of the temple.

Before ascending the ramp, Yuki is made to pull large oversized white socks over his feet and trousers. The caretakers guide everyone, one by one, onto the ramps. They remind Yuki once again that total silence is mandatory and the slightest sound, even that of a dry cough or clearing of the throat will require exiting the chamber.

Yuki treads as lightly as he possibly can on the ramp toward the upper inner chamber - Anxiously, waiting for it to disclose what it holds. The mysterious energy of the upper chamber reduces his thought frequency; his mind begins to operate on a more prolonged and higher wavelength. Yuki finds himself in a mental zone, into which he has previously seldom dared to venture.

The first impression of the inner chamber is numbing. The chamber is dim. There are twelve floor-to-ceiling steel columns with ivory-white paint. The columns, run along the periphery of the chamber and surround a central object, a radiant crystal ball.

The ball is optically perfect. The oversized glass globe rests on an intricately made gold-leaf pedestal. Through a circular crack in the middle of the ceiling, a shaft of light enters a heliostat, which directs a single ray of sunlight toward the crystal ball, in divine grace.

When the lights are switched off, the only light source is the single ray of the sun being streamed into the room by the heliostat. There are two rows of seats surrounding the crystal ball. Yuki chooses to sit cross-legged on a cushion in the outer row as it offers a backrest. Yuki is permitted to practice seated meditation for the next ten minutes and has to remain still to prevent the rustling sound of his clothes, he struggles to control his instincts to scratch and twitch. Within seconds, with all sound sources turned off, the chamber is tranquil and peaceful.

In the very first minutes, Yuki cannot find the right posture. He fidgets, and he adjusts his legs several times. His tailbone and lower back begin to throb - they need a thicker cushion. But he eventually settles down and begins to concentrate. Yuki focuses his attention, first on a mantra and then on his breathing. Later he tries to focus on nothing and eliminate all thoughts. It is impossible. His mind wanders, continually wrestling with distracting thoughts. He is failing at the simple task of being able to do nothing.

He is part of a large group in the inner chamber. With his eyes shut, he feels the stillness in the air and feels all alone in the surrounding soundlessness. He starts to feel a strange sense of drift and separation. At the same time, he becomes intensely aware of every sound, every vibration, even the movement of air and odors in the room.

It is difficult. He feels an itch on the back of his palm and scratches it very softly and carefully. The scratching sound alters the resonance of the silence. It is a much louder sound than he has ever heard the sound scratching makes. He is amazed to discover how coarse the sound of even a slight scratch truly is.

He stops instantly, wondering if the others in the room could hear it.

Yuki refocuses on his attempt to meditate. He relinquishes the control he is trying to exercise on his mind. He decides to observe his thoughts that pass by without dwelling on any of them in particular.

Yuki continues this for seven to eight minutes, and then he loses himself for a brief time in this silent prison. Silence seems to be the vital ingredient that helps him meditate. The silence begins to have its transformative effect as clarity starts dripping into his mind.

Yuki senses calm energy with his eyes shut. It is not surreal or humbling but cathartic. His mind has been reframed from a hermetically sealed echo chamber of anxiety into a pond with still waters. The experience is regenerative, and it steadies his mind. It is the first time in his life he has experienced silence to this degree. The serenity is unmatched.

Once Yuki opens his eyes, he continues to gaze at the crystal ball for the remaining minutes.

When the light turn-off and turn-on twice, it's time to exit. Yuki does not want to leave this heavenly feeling of the upper meditation hall. It is here that he has taken the first step to feeling his zen.

As he leaves the temple, Yuki becomes unhinged. His confusion disappears, and his mind delinks from the anger that had overtaken him during the divorce. Yuki feels detached from his thoughts. There is clarity and joy. Relieved, Yuki can hope to build himself back into a happy person. Yuki feels gratitude, and he begins to wonder. What was the secret of this temple? How did it manage to offer tranquillity and immense comfort? Why did it appeal to him: someone who is spiritually coarse and finds meditation unpleasant?

The answer to these questions Yuki believes is *silence*.

Silence performed an alchemical trick that forced Yuki to face his suffering and overcome it. Did silence help Yuki turn muck into gold?

Yuki wonders, is silence a condition that enables happiness or is it the elusive key to unlocking happiness?

Did silence center him? Did it draw all the energy back into him? Did It preserve, restore, and heal? Did it renew his soul?

All Yuki knows is that ten minutes of real silence did the trick, to make him pivot in a new direction. By chance or choice, silence proved to be a new life partner. Silence has no real property; it cannot be measured in decibels or quantified with weight, color, or size attributes.

In many ways, it is empty, void like a vacuum that fills the universe, but to Yuki, it was full of answers.

The temple was the sum of all goodness.

Yuki, grateful for his discovery, in the weeks that follow, comes up with a novel idea for a restaurant. He decides to open a silent restaurant, called the Zazen Cafe. Yuki would serve fresh homemade minimalist Japanese meals, making customers start their meals with a short meditation in *silence*. He would then read a thought of the day, followed by an explanation of the ingredients used and the preparation technique of the food. All patrons would be required to eat in total silence. Yuki believes mindful eating, by thinking about what they eat in silence, would engage all of their senses to truly appreciate what they are eating.

** *The 'Maitri Mandir,' in Auroville, Pondicherry, literally means the 'Temple of the Mother.' However, Yuki chose to describe it as the 'Mind Temple' based on his personal experience.*

@Cafe

Moderator, 'Yes, and the book is soon to be turned into a motion picture.'

Notable novelist, Simon Winchester accepts the compliment and, as someone who is never short of words, begins to unpack the fascinating backstory behind the book.

Rekha, sitting in the second to last row at this literature festival, on a crisp winter afternoon is impressed at the speed with which the author delivers his responses, in such masterfully crafted sentences and with impeccable diction. The author intrigues her, and she knows she must buy his book. When Rekha discloses her liking for the man to the two older Australian ladies sitting beside her, they inform her that if she is enjoying what she hears then she should buy the author's other book, *The Map that changed the world*.

Rekha buys both books at the makeshift bookstore that has been set up for the festival. At the book signing tent, she even succeeds in procuring the author's inscription on the flyleaf of both books. Rekha believes signed copies establish a personal connection with an author and moves such books to the top of her reading list. In the week that follows, Rekha reads *The Professor and the Madman*. A nifty tale about the compilation of the Oxford English Dictionary. The book has murder and madness and displays the author's love of words, all ingredients that make it an enjoyable read. She shelves the other book, a six-hundred page literary undertaking, in the hope of reading it at a later date. Rekha dislikes reading books by the same author in quick succession, for she knows the novelty wears off a little more with each successive book.

A year later, Rekha finally decides to carry the six-hundred-page book to a coffee shop, in an attempt to begin reading it for a second dose of Simon Winchester. On reading the back cover and the introduction of *The Map that changed the world* she has an inkling, that the book's subject matter may be of little interest to her. Rekha had hoped, based on the book's title, the book would be about the discovery of an elusive, secret map that holds the location of an extravagant treasure. It might include a relentless chase, a compelling story about a pursuit with a compulsive plot. The book, however, is about the creation of the first geological map of England, during the Age of Enlightenment. As Rekha begins to read, she discovers the extensively researched book is well-written and probably meant for someone interested in geology. It reads like an article published in a scientific journal.

Rekha wonders if she will ever get through to the end of the book. The book is confusing and filled with scientific jargon. The protagonist, William Smith, is obsessed with strata and rock and tracing the placement of fossils, which he uncovers in his excavations. What keeps Rekha interested is the author's writing style so she needs to get over her lethargy. She decides to at least make a fair attempt to read a part of the book.

She adopts the 'baby steps' method. She decides to read the book at her neighborhood coffee shop and not at home. The casual ambiance and the on-and-off distractions in a cafe might lighten the text's serious tone. She plans to read it on her free afternoons, only twenty pages in one sitting, no more. She refuses to subject herself to the pressure of finishing the book. Even if she decides to abandon the book midway, that would be okay. But she decides she would do her best to try and reach the last page of the book.

Rekha has a penchant for analyzing irrelevant information and deriving pointless conclusions so she starts to compute the actual cost of her reading plan. If she sets a target of 20 pages for every visit to a coffee shop, which means she would need thirty visits in all, each visit will require a tall Sumatra pour-over, as well as transportation to and from home. On every other visit, she might also need an occasional snack, a blueberry parfait, or a strawberry brioche. And, occasionally, she may even buy a latte for an intriguing stranger or an old friend, whom she might unexpectedly encounter at the cafe.

It is during her fifth visit and only eighty pages into the book that she strikes up a conversation with a young girl sitting by herself at a table beside her.

Rekha has noticed her on her previous visits. The young girl always seemed to be consumed by her laptop and submerged in her earbuds, sending off a "leave me alone to my own devices - laptop, phone, earbud" vibe. Her dress is a white satin outfit with a sleeveless blouse. Her fair complexion stands in sharp contrast to her jet-black hair, which she has allowed to fall freely over her bare shoulders. She wears little makeup. She has the blessing of perfect skin, flawless in tone and complexion, hydrated, moisturized, and full of collagen.

In the past, neither Rekha nor the girl had attempted any sort of interaction - no eye contact and no greeting. Today is different. There is a mutual feeling in the air to initiate a conversation, as though both were struck by a wave of congeniality. They strike a friendly conversation asking about each other. It becomes interesting when they start to inquire about each other's lives. As the delightful chatter progresses, moods elevate, and Rekha decides to buy this young stranger a coffee, much against the girls' insistence on buying her own coffee.

When the coffees arrive, like every coffee snob, Rekha inspects it for the perfection of proportion -

flavor, freshness, and color. The coffee grind is rich and deep, slightly burnt and bitter, and over-roasted. She is not sure if the coffee deserves her nod.

Rekha checks the bill lying on the serving tray. She lowers her readers to be able to read the amount on the bill. The grand total - the sum of various taxes and surcharges distracts her. Without paying much attention to what her new young friend is talking about, something about a cafe in France, Rekha starts running the numbers in her head.

Purchase price of the book: Rs 600

Reading twenty pages are read per visit

The cost of a tall/black pour-over is Rs 300

Require thirty visits to complete the book

Cost of reading book = 600 + 30X300 = Rs 9600

Simple arithmetic brings the total cost to a

staggering Rs 10800/

Or 18 times the cost of the book.

(Not including the occasional cruffins, muffins, and generous gifts of latte to newly acquired acquaintances nor the transportation cost.)

However, before Rekha can compute the yearly cost of reading books in a cafe, she is interrupted by the young girl, who insists that she needs to pay for her own coffee. Given her meagre twenty-four years of existence, her affectionate nature, and her show of interest, Rekha reassures the girl that she doesn't need to pay, and a simple thank you for the coffee will suffice.

It is 3 pm on a Wednesday and the cafe is abuzz with people. Outside, in glorious sunshine on the patio, some people are smoking while crows sweep up the crumbs on the floor.

Inside, the smell of coffee wafts in the air, and synthesized versions of Tom Petty and James Taylor songs pipe through the in-wall speakers. The air conditioner vents belch out ice-cold air. Four to five customers are waiting in the queue at the cash registers. Each customer is taking longer than is usual in such shops to decipher the elaborate menu printed on the wall. For a cup of freshly brewed coffee, the customers have to choose between a filter, an Americano, or a pour-over. Each of the coffees is offered in various beans: Italian, Verona, or Kenya. The trained-to-upsell cafe staff, is bombarding every customer with an endless number of names of flavors and size options.

On the corner table, three twenty-somethings are occupying too much space and have been creating a ruckus for the last hour. They are engaged in a game of mono-deal. Seemingly out of place in a cafe and after an exhausting school day, a mother has decided to treat her two kids, both below the age of ten, to an iced frappuccino. They are seated beside Rekha. Rekha and the young girl concur in a whisper that a dose of sugary coffee as an after-school snack in a cafe may not be the best choice for children this young.

Rekha tells her companion, "For my generation, an after-school snack was a glass of cold milk at home."

The young girl tells Rekha that, "'For me, it was milk and, on some days, French fries at McDonald's."

The young girl asks if Rekha likes to write, if Rekha likes to read and if Rekha likes to travel. Rekha's responses are "Yes", "Yes", "Yes." Rekha does have her laptop open in front of her, alongside her coffee and her book. Rekha is in her mid-fifties, with reading glasses placed on her forehead and dressed in a baggy linen shirt. She presents herself as an author in the making. Rekha tells the girl how she wishes to compile ten short stories in the current year. The short stories are about her travels to the south of France and Italy.

The young girl asks - "so did you travel alone?"

Rekha replies - "yes I did, as I have gotten older, I prefer to do so."

Rekha can tell by the girl's look of amazement that she is impressed by the fact that Rekha prefers to travel alone. The young girl immediately continues by saying that she, despite her inexperience and much against her parent's will, prefers the same. She had gone on a solo trip to Paris last year.

The girl is twenty-four, but she left home at seventeen to study in London. Currently, she makes a living by working part-time for a travel magazine and part-time for the avant-garde British Wire, a music magazine. At times, she writes about traveling to different places across the world. At times she reviews international music. She turns her laptop toward Rekha to show the article she is currently writing. She is also working on a novel.

The young girl says, "I began by typing this essay first in the Helvetica font and then decided to use an elegant cursive font like Apple Chicanery. For some reason, the font does impact your thinking and your style of writing. This font makes me feel like it is handwritten, and I have something important, even noteworthy, to write about." They both chuckle.

Their laughter is interrupted by a member of the cafe staff, carrying a tray full of bite-size samples of an apple turnover in mini paper cups. They both sample the servings. They wonder if this is how the Cafe gets rid of the food that is about to go bad.

Drawing back to their conversation, Rekha and the young girl decide that they have a lot in common - a universal disdain for Bollywood movies, and a common liking for writers living in London and New York.

Rekha likes the girl's open and chatty nature. They concur that Bollywood with its over-the-top emotional sagas, intolerable humor, unnecessary song and dance routines, simple repetitive plots, and the sheer three-hour-long marathon running time should pay its audience's to sit through its movies.

Coincidently the last Bollywood movie both of them had watched was *Secret Superstar*. Both of them were turned off by the movie's ending. The little girl in the film, who came from modest beginnings faces sever opposition from her father but becomes a superstar by posting anonymous music videos on the internet. Rekha's companion wishes the movie had an understated ending, where it would have been sufficient for the young girl to pursue her dream, undeterred, and not necessarily achieve stardom.

The young girl raises some important questions - Does one only realize one's dream if one attains some amount of greatness? Or is it more important to pursue one's dreams for personal contentment?

They both question the emphasis on success and how it is measured in today's society. Why does success need to be measured with the obvious parameters of awards, prizes, wealth, etc. Can contentment, satisfaction, fulfillment, and mental peace provide a similar sense of success?

But no, Rekha reminds the young girl, this is Bollywood, and exaggeration is their key ingredient for movie-making.

They both dislike movie endings where good wins over evil, the boy gets the girl, or a superhero saves the world. They both like movies with controversial endings, endings that surprise you, or make you question things or upset you. Their favorite Hollywood movies are *The Sixth Sense*, *The Usual Suspects*, *Brokeback Mountain*.

In a very short time, Rekha discovers that despite their age difference, the conversation between them flows naturally. The young girl, like Rekha declares that she is a devoted reader of writers from London and New York. Rekha agrees - in fact, she believes that it is mandatory to relocate to London or New York to make it as a writer in English. Having lived in both cities Rekha tells the girl, that great historical works of literature have been received primarily from the minds of authors living in London and New

York. The two cities, despite being ridiculously expensive for a notoriously un-lucrative profession, are still the best breeding grounds for literary creativity. Both cities have produced writers of much acclaim.

Rekha, having lived in America for the past twenty-five years, and the young girl having been educated in London, both still feel very Indian. And, both aspire to be Indian writers in English.

They agree that such writers generally do not align with the bloodlines of writers from London and New York. The fluency of thought, the efficiency of grammar, and the ability to twist the English language comfortably, for such writers is largely because they have spoken and written in English for many more centuries than their Indian counterparts. It is this limitation of the language not being in the genes, in the bones, or in the blood, that are the disadvantageous pursuing a career as an Indian author writing in English. Rekha makes a few comparisons to prove her point - Chetan Bhagat versus Alan Hollinghurst and Amish Tripathi versus Andrew Sean Greer. Rekha is aware that it is unfair to make such comparisons but she tells the young girl that it only means one thing: that they will have to work ten times as hard as their American and British counterparts.

For a second time, a member of the Cafe staff, carrying a tray full of cookie crumble mocha in mini paper cups, interrupts their conversation. He asks them if they would like to sample. They both try the delectable mini-portion of the concoction. They wonder if this is a method adopted by the Cafe to suggest buying another drink.

Rekha and the young girl discover that they share a common quirk, which is for the hyper cleanliness of bathrooms. According to both of them, the floor must always be dry, the tiles always look new, the toilet has to be spotless, and the air free of any repugnant odors. The free end of the toilet paper should be rolled over and not under the bar. Rekha concludes that a similar sense of hygiene is a rare to find in another person. This only proves one thing: they are very similar in a lot of ways.

Now Rekha is feeling extremely comfortable talking to her new friend. The young girl resumes the conversation by telling Rekha that she is writing a biography of sorts. The young girl admits that she is too young to write a biopic. Her new work is about how an orphan, who sets out on a journey to discover her roots finds herself. The process reveals her insecurities and character flaws both of which she has been refusing to accept. The narrative centers around how the girl's life is driven by aspirations but thwarted by reality and her inability to speak the truth.

She informs Rekha that she has submitted the first draft of the book to a publisher and her proposal is under review. If all went well, the book will soon be published. The feedback from her publisher is that the draft is generally pleasing and what she has to say and how she says it is what many young adults want to hear.

"Wow," Rekha begins to wonder, "The young girl has procured a publishing deal at twenty-four! That is impressive." Being twice her age, Rekha has spent two years to finalize her short stories.

Rekha soon finds out from the conversation that follows, that the young girl's talents are not just limited to writing a novel; she has ventured into playwriting as well. She has worked on two Broadway plays with none other than Patrick Stewart, who is sponsoring her next play. Did Rekha hear correctly? Patrick Stewart of *StarTrek* fame?

Last November, when *Game of Thrones* was at its prime viewing peak, the young girl said she had had the privilege of meeting its author, known by his initials GRRM (George R R Martin). Rekha tells her that she always thought he was British, but the young girl informs Rekha that he is American. She even had the opportunity to ask GRRM why he did not kill the likable character of John Snow much earlier in the series.

To even think of suggesting a change in the storyline to GRRM is unfathomable. The first seeds of doubt about the veracity of what the young girl is saying begin to germinate in Rekha's head. Rekha is thinking, "Is this for real? If it is, then this is just marvelous!"

The young girl's grandiose statement has put both of them in a fantastic mood, and Rekha is in awe of this young girl's mind and she wants to continue to prod it and have fun with it, a little longer. But

Rekha's suspicion rises again. Is the young girl just making stuff up, or did some of the stuff she's been talking about really happen?

A man, Rekha's age, taps her on her left shoulder to gain her attention. He has two other younger men following him, all in suits. From the first impression of them, Rekha guesses a job interview is about to commence. The older gentleman who is in charge asks her if she would be willing to swap seats; Rekha declines by shaking her head and without saying a word. Then he asks Rekha if she can move over, as they can share the table with her and the young girl. Rekha obliges. From sitting side by side Rekha will now have to sit facing the young girl. Rekha shifts her coffee, laptop, book, and phone to the young girl's table. The young girl accommodates her. The man is now seated on Rekha's side of the table with the two job applicants facing him. Rekha is sitting opposite and facing the young girl, at the same table.

From being fond of writing in the English language, the conversation moves to the ability to speak other languages. The young girl informs Rekha that she speaks four languages, besides the obvious languages Hindi and English. She speaks

French and Italian fluently. She had mastered Italian through a rocket Italian online course in two months. Rekha wonders if that is even possible to be able to learn Italian without ever having been to Italy or having conversed with a native speaker. The young girl claims to have learned French through immersion. At twenty-two, she lived in France for six months. To hear French all day and attempt to speak it every day resulted in her absorbing French just by living a normal life in France. Language learning came naturally to her. "To accumulate a language," the young girl says, "One needs to invest not just the head but the heart too." Rekha thinks to herself; *she is a gifted hyperpolyglot.*

Rekha had supposed learning a new language one needed to have hours of practice, practice, practice. After two weeks in Brazil, she could hone in on only a couple of phrases in Portuguese.

Rekha now seriously starts to wonder. Rekha silently begins to evaluate the young girl's language ability. Rekha starts paying close attention to everything she is saying, and she picks up a lot of errors in how the girl communicates in English. She mispronounces words - Rekha can pardon that, but her using unnecessary *s*'s after particular words, (such as when she said, "Need a new SIMs card") and repeatedly using 'like' as a filler, is unpardonable. Making such basic errors in a language you claim to love and have spoken for the last twenty-four years is unacceptable. Rekha begins to question her proficiency in other languages but has no toolkit to put her through a test. But then again, maybe she possesses specialized neurology that is well-suited for mastering languages, or probably she just has superhuman skills in making things up.

Once again, a tray of food is being served, offered through the cafe. The young lady of the cafe staff, dressed in a black shirt, green apron, and a baseball cap, asks Rekha in her honey-toned Indian accent. If she wants to sample a new addition to the menu, the "Chicken Empadana," Rekha snickers, being much older than the waitress, she feels she has the right to correct her, in her mix of Indian and American accents, and tell her, it is "Chicken Empanada, the N before the D." The cafe lady takes no offense. She continues to smile as she has been trained to, all part of the overarching goal to provide excellent customer service.

Rekha asks her to repeat after her, the waitress tries for a second time but still says, "Chicken Empadana." They burst out laughing together. Oh well! Is this a demonstration of language not being in your bloodstream?

Rekha's new young friend is suddenly distracted by a message on her phone. Rekha is guessing it is probably a forward on Whatsapp, an instant message on Facebook, a DM on Instagram, a tweet, or a notification from Bumble. The application is of little consequence, but the message in a particular inbox requires the young girl's urgent, undivided attention. Listening to the muffled soundtrack of *A Million Dreams*, Rekha can see it's a video forward of a scene from *The Greatest Showman* the movie. The young girl watches the video intently and complains about the WIFI speed and the forced advertising before the clip. The barrage of advertising is upsetting her. Rekha can see it in her facial expressions. The young girl says, "It is excessive, relentless without subtlety." Rekha could not agree more - "And non-stop," she adds.

The young girl seems a little disappointed with the clip, without sharing any information regarding it. She says, "You only live once and you have to follow your dreams because no one else is going to follow them for you." "Following your dreams is a very millennial attribute," Rekha adds. Rekha informs her that when she was her age, all she did was a job, in fact, any job, at times the very first job she could get, to pay her bills, and in all those years she never felt guilty about suppressing her inner desires or dreams. For twenty-five years, year after year, she sold her soul to a corporation, she traded her passion for practicality, her dreams for stability, saving, and investing till one day she was able to achieve financial independence. Rekha admits that at fifty-five, having secured a nifty little nest egg, she now finds herself in a better position to follow her dreams.

The young girl disagrees, She says, "It is essential to enjoy what you do or life shall just pass you by." She rightly doubts if Rekha has enjoyed the work she has done until now.

The free coffee, samples of the apple turnover, cookie crumble mocha, and the chicken empanada shifts the young friend into a new gear and makes her irredeemably talkative. She continues as an unstoppable bandwagon.

The young girl claims that money means nothing to her. While she was in Paris, when she was short on cash, she would buy a box of paints, make a painting, and sell it to one of the multitude of galleries along the Seine. *She is a painter too!* Rekha thinks to herself, Rekha has seen so many struggling painters on the sidewalks of Paris who can barely sell a work of art for ten euros - and then, only after much bargaining with a tourist hungry for French art.

Rekha soon figures out that the young girl is also overly confident about her looks. She believes she looks much younger and a lot healthier than other girls her age. On one of her auditions (oh yes, she's also an actress!), she informed Rekha that she was asked to play the part of a sixteen year-old in a Bollywood movie while a sixteen-year-old actor was deemed more suitable to play the role of a working girl in her late twenties.

Rekha thinks, *"that in appearance, she has everything one wants, and some things, in fact, that are more than any person could ever want - free spirit, risk-taker, go-getter, all qualities cultivated with such ease."*

The conversation is now one-sided. The young girl subjects Rekha to her fantastical monologues. She tells Rekha about her plans and her resolutions, her talents, accomplishments, aspirations, and desires - all without pause. Her achievements are a result of a serendipitous meshing of one set of skills with another, a co-mingling of fantasy and absurdity.

Last, among of her many talents, she states that she can predict the method of one's death. *"How is that possible to be able to foretell a farewell to life?"* Rekha wonders. Rekha as she sits still with her pupils dilated, shaking her head from side to side.

For Rekha, this is it. It is time to leave. She has lost all interest in the young girl's skewed sense of reality. The little coffee that Rekha has left is cold and bitter and sits at the bottom of the mug. It's time to leave. At first, Rekha excuses herself to go to the washroom. When she returns, she thanks the young girl for an engaging conversation, packs her book and laptop in her carry bag, and walks out of the cafe.

As Rekha leaves the cafe, she can only surmise that the encounter should be considered a classic in the annals of meeting strangers in cafes.

Rekha never could have imagined that one human being could engage in so many pursuits. Rekha wonders where life will lead the young girl next with her breadth of intellect. In her frenzied claims, the world always seemed to be at her fingertips, at her beck and call.

The young girl's prodigious imagination seemed to view the world with a perspective that harbored intellectual freedom, free to imagine that anything is possible. She was optimistic that in due course the perspective will help her achieve astonishing things.

Rekha had gone to the cafe, after all, to feel like she was a part of this world. The young girl had managed to paint a very ingenious but to say the least, delusional picture the left Rekha questioning the world she was part of!

Hoodie$

An airport is a busy place. Amid all the people rushing to find their departure gates, with their bags in tow, Kabir approaches the long queue at the boarding gate of his flight. The gates to the aircraft are still closed but the passengers have eagerly queued up to board the plane. They are vying to complete the onboarding process quickly and ahead of others by sneaking into the gaps in the queue left by daydreaming passengers. The audacity! Kabir walks by the empty chairs in the boarding area. He sees a young boy still slumped in the chair, with his legs spread wide, all by himself. Choosing comfort over style, the boy is wearing Khaki shorts and has a black hoodie pulled over his head. The hood envelops most of his face. He is consumed by his phone.

Some people board the plane last. They trust the system. They travel light and do not fret about finding space in the overhead bins.

The dire possibility of an Instagram reel distracting him longer than it should, makes Kabir think the boy might just miss his flight. Even if that were to happen, Kabir knows the boy would not stress. He is cool, perhaps too cool for his own good. "To each his own," Kabir says to himself and proceeds to embark on the aircraft, ignoring the boy.

Standing by his seat, Kabir puts his bags in the overhead bin and slips a pack of mouth fresheners into the pocket of the seat in front of him. Passengers are blocking the aisleway, taking what seems like an increasingly long amount of time to stow their luggage, oblivious to the passengers with seats in the back rows trying to pass through.

The flight attendants stand indifferently by the plane's exit doors, not concerned if passengers can find space above their seats for their carry-ons. They believe that things would eventually normalize. The flight is already forty minutes late and people are beginning to get a little testy. A passenger throws herself onto the seat in an ill-tempered huff, in the row in front of Kabir. Flying is undeniably stressful and fraught with inconvenience for most. The seating inside the aircraft is clustered into two-four-two seats in each row. Kabir is on the aisle seat of row twenty-two of the two-seat cluster. The window seat next to him is still unoccupied. Kabir is apprehensive about who would end up sitting next to him, but today his stars are in order. An extremely sophisticated lady politely asks him to let her in. She is of mixed origins from central Asia. Smilingly, Kabir obliges and lets his soon-to-be seat buddy pass by. Shooting the breeze as they travel the five-hour flight in her company, after all, might just end up being bearable without annoying the heck out of either of them.

Feeling relieved, Kabir settles in. By now the last of the passengers are trickling through the front door of the aircraft and the aisleways have cleared. Then, just as it seems the boarding is complete, Kabir sees the young boy come walking down the aisle. It is the middle of winter, and the boy is dressed in shorts and a black sweatshirt, but that might just be his airport look. The boy catches Kabir staring and simply smiles. It is just a smile, but Kabir reads into it – it is warm, welcoming, and inviting. As the boy walks by, Kabir's eyes follow him to see where he would end up sitting.

The boy proceeds to sit in the four-seat cluster in the row behind Kabir. Kabir turns around and sees that not only are the seats where the boy is sitting, unoccupied, but they also have extra legroom. There are no other passengers besides the boy in the four-seat row. Without thinking, unprompted, as though driven by a higher force, Kabir gets up, walks back to the row, and says out loud, "Wow this legroom is nice."

The boy instantly replies with his warm welcoming smile,

"Come sit here."

"Maybe after the aircraft is airborne," Kabir says.

Flight attendants sometimes object to passenger movements before take-offs. There are always some last-minute stragglers from connecting flights that roll in to occupy seemingly empty seats.

The boy brimming with confidence and good cheer assures Kabir that nothing of the sort would happen and the boarding is complete. In an act of unrequired kindness, he moves a seat over clearing the aisle seat for Kabir to sit in.

How could Kabir decline this boy-with-the-beaming-smile's offer? Kabir immediately takes the aisle seat. They are now sitting next to each other, in adjacent seats, even when there is an option to leave an empty seat between them. The boy is Kabir's new seat buddy, and Kabir has no guilt about infringing on his personal space. The aircraft starts to taxi toward the take-off runway. The flight attendant, standing right beside Kabir, starts making the safety announcements in a foreign language. Safety is the last thing on Kabir's mind. Kabir is looking for a pretext to start a conversation. From the corner of his eye, Kabir sees the boy set his telephone to airplane mode, a measure mandatory on any flight, and slip the phone into the kangaroo pocket of his hoodie. Kabir is pleased. Now, at least, there won't be any unwanted cell phone interruptions.

Never struggling to come up with something to say or ask, Kabir showers his new companion with a barrage of inquiries. Being close to twice his age, Kabir thinks the boy would be most likely at some point to ask Kabir to mind his own business or resort to a quip, to all his prying questions, such as, "What is it to you?" Kabir probably deserves it for being invasive and slightly creepy.

But the boy does not retreat, Kabir can see his devilishly handsome Iberian face, even though the fair skin of half his face is covered by the hoodie. His full lips are his most prominent feature. Every time he speaks his lips part to reveal white well-spaced, teeth. Being relatively easy on the eyes, Kabir finds it easy to hear him speak about himself.

Talking to the boy is effortless. There seems to be none of the barriers one often finds between strangers who meet on a plane. As the conversation rolls along at a natural speed, Kabir notices the boy's bare legs under his shorts. Even though the boy says he loves to play soccer, his skinny legs undercut that claim.

Cooped up together in the metal tube 30,000 feet in the sky, the boy willingly reveals that, he drives a Mercedez cabriolet and loves making money. He has invested his money in an off-plan real estate development and the developer assures him that his investment will bring a lucrative return in a very short term.

Kabir, who owns a real estate agency, advises against buying into the false promises of real estate promoters. The boy assures Kabir that with the help of his father, he would do the necessary due diligence before closing the deal.

Kabir wants to know where his companion is from and what his father does for a living. The boy answers that "Going back home to *Balencia.*"

Did he just mispronounce the v in *Valencia* as a b? Kabir is confused by the garbled mispronunciation for he clearly heard him say *Balencia.*

Back home the boy is heir to a Spanish tile-making company, that uses clay to create ceramic azulegos. The company has recently decided that it is time to diversify into real estate and make money from brick and mortar.

Kabir agreeably says, "Being passionate about making money is a good ambition to have at your age.

For you know what, money talks and bullshit walks. Being rich makes misery more enjoyable!"

Much to Kabir's surprise, the boy loves Kabir's pithy statement and instantly tells him to repeat it so that he can make a mental note. Then he decides to note it on his phone for permanence and future reference. Along with the quote he saves Kabir's name and telephone number. While this transpires, Kabir notices his companion's clothes are top brand and the Hublot on his wrist has 18K gold numerals.

The bright afternoon sun is streaming in through the porthole on the far right. The aircraft is now at cruising altitude, and it is beginning to feel a little chilly inside. The drop in temperature makes Kabir drowsy and he wants to take a nap. So, Kabir stretches across the three seats with the boy's permission, and the boy says he would do the same by just stretching on his single seat. As Kabir lies beside him on the three seats, he cannot help but notice the boy's bare legs. He senses the drop in cabin temperature triggering a chill. Kabir offers his jacket to throw over his legs, but the boy says he would ask for a blanket. But none of the airline staff is in sight and in the next few moments, the boy dozes off.

As Kabir lies beside him, the smell of the boy's breath stays with him. Every time he spoke, leaning into Kabir, a whiff of his breath swept over Kabir's face. It is rare to like another human's exhaled air, but yes, Kabir likes how the boy's breath feels on him.

Kabir has an impulse to touch the boy. Kabir knows the boy has entertained an interaction, less out of interest and more out of politeness. If Kabir did dare to touch the boy inappropriately. The boy most likely would shriek in disgust and abrasively dismiss Kabir's affections.

Kabir wants to hold the boy's hand and draw him closer. If that were to happen, the boy in all likelihood would break into a nervous sweat and feel repulsed.

Kabir's mind starts racing, and loses all inhibitions, Kabir starts fantasizing.

If Kabir were to drift his finger along the face and trace it down the neckline, the boy would probably pummel Kabir with his fists a dozen times or punch

Kabir in the face or push Kabir to the floor and beat him to a pulp — the outcomes are limitless and dreadful. Kabir, in his fantasy, wants his advances to conclude with a peck on the boy's full set of lips. If he were to do so, Kabir can see the boy walking away swearing and cussing, wanting Kabir to get out of his sight. This perhaps would be a justification for the second beating. Falling prey to the fantasy of a romantic frisson while being airborne and plagued by sexually intrusive thoughts, Kabir fears his imagination crossing a line. There is little risk in imagining what Kabir wants to do as long as he only *imagines* it. However, Kabir does not stop, he lets his imagination run loose and wild, and he feels all the sensations that he desires. Reality would most likely only complicate matters. Kabir does not want to restrict himself to the narrow parameters that reality offers.

Kabir's devious thoughts stem from an overload of emotions. Holding the boy's hand, drawing him close, burying his neck in his arms, squeezing the boy into himself. Undressing him. Caressing those clean-shaven legs, wrapping them around his waist, licking every inch of his beautiful youthful body. He feels warm and starts to feel heady as his imaginings grow raunchier. Kabir is enjoying his unique metamorphic experience, sitting next to someone who has managed to improve his life in a matter of minutes.

As Kabir tries to nap next to the boy, he plays out all his fantasies without guilt. As long as the boy does not figure out what is running through his mind, he is safe. The boy cannot censor Kabir's thoughts. Kabir has no reason to prevent himself from enjoying the fantasy, so Kabir carries on: imagining a vacation together but knowing that the magic of someone new never lasts long, Kabir also imagines a breakup. Though short-lived, Kabir's happiness knows no bounds. It is highly unlikely that anything would materialize between them in real life.

Failing to fall asleep, Kabir decides to sit up. The boy is still asleep next to Kabir, still with no blanket. Kabir has the best feeling: he immediately walks to the rear of the aircraft to fetch a blanket. When he gets back to his seat, he unfolds the blanket and throws it over the bare legs. The boy opens his eyes, barely visible from the hoodie now covering most of his face, and softly says, "Thank you."

Kabir looks into the boy's eyes - to see if the boy has an inkling of what he has been thinking about. Those deep blue eyes peeking back at Kabir from the shadow of the hoodie seemed to say, "Carry on…"

Kabir sits back in his seat and the aircraft begins its final descent.

As the plane thunders down the runway while landing, Kabir and his companion sit side by side and inadvertently happen to look at each other. Kabir wants to place his hand on the boy's hand, which is resting on the armrest between them, but he lacks the courage. Their lives intersect today on the plane. Out of all the thousands of flights that are concurrently crisscrossing the skies at any given moment, Kabir feels as though his soul mate is with him on the very flight he is on. What are the odds? They speak but perhaps do not speak the same language. No lifelong bonds are formed.

Kabir asks him, under the guise of neutrality, if he slept well. He says, "ye I res," He drops the consonants at the end of the words making 'yes' and 'rest' sound like 'ye' and 'res.' Kabir and the boy decide to stay in touch. Kabir asks him a final question, to double-check if the boy had read his mind which had imagined the in-flight romance "Do you remember my name?"

The question seems to catch the boy by surprise, throws him off, and in utter confusion, Kabir's plane crush instinctively blurts out in Spanish -'como?' and bursts out laughing.

Como, in Spanish, can mean 'what?' But the boy meant to say, "No I don't remember your name." To Kabir, it meant, 'There would never be any romantic intrigue. And, that's an understatement for all that it was, it was only an intimacy prompted by proximity."

It was time to lay this to rest, for Kabir's imagination had had a good run.

Imagination is in rich luminous colors while reality is, unfortunately, black and white.

____TrAIL

On a winter day in mid-afternoon, a light breeze ruffles Rene's hair under the cobalt sky. Rene climbs the stairs of the white metal viewing platform erected at the tip of the white desert, for a 360-degree view. What he sees is stark but dazzling. A vast expanse of approximately 2900 square miles of a flat desert, encrusted with white sea salt. The far-reaching and boundless, partly a salt marsh and partly a dry desert appears inhospitable, devoid of any habitation, wildlife, or vegetation. The denuded landscape is bereft of rows of high-tension power transmission towers with their suspended electric cables, factories or farm houses, and other man-made structures that generally are scattered over barren lands.

Standing on the platform's edge, Rene breathes the clean air, which smells like well nothing at all. After breathing enough of the purified air, his chest starts to feel light. Like alabaster, the white desert is just flat and white spread over miles and miles, as far as the eye can see. It is untouched by the meddlesome nature of humanity.

Shimmering under the bright afternoon sun, the vast hollow space that fills the desert between the sky and the ground leaves Rene breathless! The levelled, uninterrupted view of the earth is uncomplicated. Rene realizes how beautiful the planet is in its natural state. Nature when left alone, appears harmonious even when harsh.

This moment on the platform is a great start to his exploration of the surrounding region, which Rene decided to visit to source locally grown, indigenous cotton for his sustainably-inspired men's clothing brand. He hires a local cab to drive to visit cotton farms and local villages to explore the various handicrafts that thrive in the region. The driver, Anwar, is a local and also an abundant source of fun facts and trivia. He promises Rene a non-touristic, off-the-beaten-path tour of native handicrafts —

mainly block-printed, hand-painted, and embroidered fabrics. Rene decides to let Anwar lead the way.

As they begin their journey, the first thing Rene notices are the numerous resorts that line the highway. All the resorts look similar, consisting of circular mud huts offering homestays.

Anwar tells Rene, "These huts are made of an earthy mix of mud and a generous portion of manure, dung from cows, horses, camels, goats, and donkeys. They are well suited to the region as they regulate the temperature, and amazingly contain no bacteria so you can enjoy disease-free living. They are a natural deterrent to scorpions and snakes, which abound in the arid landscape. Though basic in structure and furnishings the most beneficial outcome about these huts is the quality of sleep you enjoy within their walls —"uninterrupted and mood-lifting."

Rene passes a signboard that informs him that the Tropic of Cancer, an imaginary line 23 degrees above the equator circling the earth, passes through here. To date, Rene had only seen the Tropic of Cancer on maps and globes, as a line drawn with dots, dashes or the like. He asks Anwar to stop the car by the signboard. Standing there, Rene wonders, "Is there a hidden meaning to being atop such a significant latitude?" But he knows that this is just a fun fact, a bit of trivia good to know. So, he urges Anwar to carry on.

After every two-to-three kilometers, Rene notices several large milk cans abandoned by the side of the road. When he mentions this to Anwar, he is told, "The cans are left by the dairy farmers for collection by large milk amalgamators. There is never any theft here. The locals are extremely honest and trustworthy."

In his previous travels, Rene has been robbed of his wallet once and of his phone twice. Anwar's reassuring words placate his paranoia about losing his phone and wallet. Anwar tells Rene that if he were to lose them, they would most likely be returned.

Rene soon spots cotton and castor fields and herds of cattle grazing on farmlands. Then they pass gas stations selling biodiesel and eco-fuel. A local shop has a billboard that beckons you to try organic juices extracted from local fruit, such as mango and guava. A caravan of camels, led by their keeper, passes them going in the opposite direction on the road. The slow pace of their softly padded feet slows down traffic. The train of fifty dromedaries, single-humped brown camels with gigantic sable eyes staring blankly, transports Rene back in time when camels used to be a choice of transportation.

Although the landscape is bleak, the local tribes are dressed in brightly colored ethnic garb. Deep reds, bright yellows, midnight blues and indigo abound on the clothes along with elaborate embroidery stitches and rich mirrorwork decoration.

The by lanes on the highway are speckled with small villages, where the region's handicraft treasures can be discovered. As they take a detour through a village Rene sees no traffic lights, but he does notice a helmet-less scooterist greeting and shaking hands with a police officer standing on the roundabout, both indifferent to the obvious traffic violation.

There are signboards of not-for-profits plastered on the walls of houses and electric poles. These organizations have made their way into these tiny villages to promote the rich artisanal traditions of the region.

Their names are uplifting - the English translations being - Virtuous, Creativity, Intrinsic Pride, and Art Preservation. Rene feels inspired and begins to wonder what about the region do organizations want to preserve, strengthen, and promote. Are they trying to protect local heritage from vanishing into the folds of history?

This is a region whose traditions trace back to the five-thousand-year-old Harappan civilization. Descendants of farmers, weavers, ginners, hand-spinners, dyers, painters, potters, and metal workers still inhabit the area. Several tribes are pastoral, living off the surrounding grasslands and scrublands.

Rene sees potters making terracotta products, which the women paint using bamboo leaves. These fragile freshly pottered vases, planters, and saucers lie carelessly and without fuss everywhere.

In the courtyard of an old home, Rene sees a young boy stooped over, delicately, and precisely painting with acute detail on a stretched fabric extended over a small table. With his right hand, he dips a stylus in pigments made from castor oil and vegetable dyes and creates intricate motifs on the fabric – geometric flowers, peacocks, and the tree of life. Most of the artwork created is from the history of folk culture.

In the neighboring courtyard, three women are huddled over a woven bed with wooden legs, enjoying an afternoon of embroidering in the warm afternoon sun. Their embroidered trousseaus are colorfully threaded in symmetrical patterns and geometric shapes of tiny triangles, tight squares, and round buttonholes in a cross-stitch pattern.

Each house seems to specialize in an intriguing craft — camel hair weaving, making leather bags, horse belts, cushion covers, mirror frames, block-printed fabric, the list is endless.

Rene sees a thatched house its walls made of mud bricks; its pleasant aesthetic intrigues him. On its outside is a sign that says, "Organic cotton sold here."

The entry gates to the house are unlocked. Rene opens the gate and walks onto the front porch without seeking permission. No one is in sight. To his right, the area has been turned into a feedlot full of hay for the livestock. The livestock consists of two cows, and three goats — chained to tree stumps. A stray dog scampers among them.

The courtyard smells of manure, ammonia, and wood smoke. There is a biogas plant in the back, converting waste into energy. Rene senses the people who inhabit this house have a deep connection with their land and have been existing with nature for many years.

To his left, opposite the livestock area, are the living quarters. Freshly rinsed farm produce — carrots, radishes, and coriander bunches — lie sprawled, along with earthen pots that hold drinking water. A mud hearth serves as a wood stove on which a delicious local recipe is being concocted in a covered cast Iron pan. Wholesome home-cooking. Rene sees very few utensils in the kitchen area or other kitchen appliances. The simple house lacks items of modern-day comfort and luxury. A very minimalistic life is being lived here, with only a few possessions. Living in a barren desert, the locals depend on the sun, soil, and wind to eat and live.

Quriously

Rene witnesses' human beings living off the earth, first-hand.

At the back of the house is where the workshop and the store are set up. As Rene walks towards the store, he is greeted by the owner who appears out of nowhere. The owner asks Rene to remove his shoes before he enters. The store is a semi-circular room without pillars, topped with a conical straw roof. It has several wooden windows. The window frames are freshly painted with flashy motifs of flowers, birds, animals, and human figures. The store's walls are cotton white. The entire collection of mellow fabrics, mostly oatmeal-colored, is hand-folded and stacked vertically in square heaps along the base of the walls. Depending on how the warp and weave threads are interlaced, the fabric is hand-woven into a variety of weaves: thin weaves, plain weaves, twill weaves, and basket weaves.

Nature and the surrounding fields seem to influence the color tones and the subtle hues of the fabric. The fabric stacks are in neutral earth tones and woodsy browns. Scarves hang from hooks on walls, dyed in natural indigo, a characteristic color of the region, the color instills a sense of calm and confidence, typical of many blues.

Rene walks around the space in the center of the room and starts to feel the fabric. Depending on the thread count each piece has a characteristic feel, from coarse to fine. Rene picks up a swatch of the fine fabric to assess its form. It feels soft without wax or starch. It smells fresh. It is desirable. When he stands under the light, it reveals its beautiful tan color and its supreme quality.

As Rene presses the fabric between his palms, he wants to wrap his bare skin in it. It appears durable and comfy. It feels like well-washed linen, without weight. Rene begins to develop a connection with this fabric — spun thread derived from a dependable foundation of centuries-old farming techniques.

The owner in an embroidered turban, wears clothes made from the fabric that he sells. He is confident and speaks to Rene with kindness. As he unfolds roll after roll of fabric on the ground for examination, Rene browses through the wares, the owner starts to narrate the benefits of the cotton from the region. Certain facts strike a chord with Rene.

The owner proudly states, "The cotton from this region is rainfed, drought-resistant, pesticide-free, and requires little attention to grow. It is also hand spun by our artisans."

He adds, "Clothes out of this textile are free of toxic chemicals."

Rene wonders, "Is it hypoallergenic, too?" Rene's polyester gym track pant, which he has been wearing for over eight hours, is starting to feel clammy. Rene's sweat, mixed with the heat and humidity of the weather, is beginning to irritate the skin on his right calf. Even as he starts to vigorously scratch to relieve the irritation, he tries to stop himself. He knows repeated scratching will turn his skin red and bumpy and may even cause it to bleed.

The owner continues speaking about the cloth - "Wear the new fabric in the winter and the same fabric when worn and washed a few times will keep you cool in the summer."

With the fabric still in his hands, at some unspeakable level, Rene finds joy. He falls in love with the cloth. He wishes he was wearing pants made from this natural material — material, untreated with harmful chemicals, synthetic fertilizers, or pesticides and born of eco-friendly practices at all stages of turning crop to cloth. At this moment, he imagines eco-wear - clothes that balance the environment, the health of the user, and the welfare of the producer.

Rene has always believed that he should live a life that makes a positive impact on the environment. To make any significant impact, he has always felt that one needs to undertake large-scale projects for a green infrastructure requiring hefty investments. Wind farms, solar fields, electric cars, bio-fuel airplanes, and vertical agriculture are not options for individuals in which they can participate daily to contribute toward a better ecology.

Rene has wondered how he could make a difference at an individual level. Today he found his answer - from this point on he needs to start building a wardrobe with environmentally friendly clothing.

Looking back, Rene realizes that in the last ten years, he has accumulated closets full of clothes. As a child in the seventies, he stored all of his clothes, on a single shelf in a shared wardrobe with his sibling. The shelf contained school uniforms, party clothes, play clothes, socks, and undergarments. The single shelf seemed sufficient then. However, in the last twenty years, his clothing pile had become so large that it has filled two wardrobes, in two houses, in two different cities.

Rene has a moment of reckoning: he has too many clothes! He has never given thought to where or how they were manufactured, what the fabric blends are and if they are treated with toxic chemicals or colored with synthetic dyes, or where they end up when he discards them — The ocean? A landfill? Or an incinerator?

A few years ago, Rene had been part of a local beach cleaning initiative. Every Sunday morning, he would clean the neighborhood beach by picking up garbage by hand. The assortment of garbage that he picked up consisted of plastic bottles, wrappers, shoes, burlap bags, and lots and lots of clothes deeply sunk in the sand. It was back-breaking work to pull the clothes from the sand. Jackets, and pants were so deeply buried that it required the strength of two or more individuals to get them out. The impact excessive clothing could have on the beach was alarming.

The sheer amount of clothes that needed to be removed from the beach made Rene aware that huge amounts of clothes were being carelessly discarded into the ocean. This fact was a direct outcome of over-production and excessive consumption.

Rene thought to himself that he was somewhat guilty for the present situation. He rarely wore any particular item of clothing more than six or seven times, after which it found its way to a stack in the back rows of his wardrobe or hung drooping on a hanger for months. He re-wore too few items and never thought of recycling them. Unused clothing eventually ended up in the trash.

Rene bought clothes based on brand, price, color, style, seasonality, and current trends or according to how they would look on his body. He had a thousand reasons to buy new clothes, and he bought too many. He usually bought on impulse. He bought just because an item was on sale or when he felt he was getting a good deal. Realizing that at times the best deal was no deal at all.

By choosing clothes with natural fibers such as organic cotton, Rene feels he can now contribute daily to the betterment of the planet.

He concludes that it is important to think about what one wears — what it is made of and where it comes from.

From this point forward Rene decides he is going to save up and spend right, he will buy less but buy better, and buy only if he needs it. He will, in short, spend his money on the change he wants to see.

And when possible, he will only wear the colors of nature, made from material in its least altered state.

When Rene returns to his car, the sun has set, and it's pitch dark on the street. As he sits in the back, he hears Anwar say,

"Looks like you bought what you like. This is what is called the handicraft trail."

Rene says, "You are lucky you live among a vibrant tradition."

Rene shuts his eyes and an image of the white desert flashes passes by in his mind. He has this feeling that the image of this white desert will stay with him for a long time to come.

He is beginning to like his newfound natural vibe.

About The Author

Vinnie has always turned to writing during the grace periods of his life. He used his Master's Degree in Business Administration from UCLA, to make a naked grab for money from American Capitalism and Innovation for twenty-five years. After this, he swapped the fifth-avenue banker lifestyle for that of a literary observer.

Vinnie is no stranger to feeling like a stranger. For the majority of his adult life, he has been an immigrant, a foreigner, and an outsider. He has lived unnoticed in Luxembourg, Boston, Wilmington, Los Angeles, and New York and wandered, at times feeling lost in various cities, surveying people, places, and things.

About The Author

Vinnie believes in serial entrepreneurship, keeping our beaches clean, enjoys occasional math, and craves a kind of wanderlust and a wish to travel back in time to simpler days. He is influenced heavily by immaculate writing and flawless prose.

This is his first publication of short stories.

www.ingramcontent.com/pod-product-compliance
Lightning Source LLC
LaVergne TN
LVHW041712070526
838199LV00045B/1314